Picture the Middle Ages

The Middle Ages Resource Book

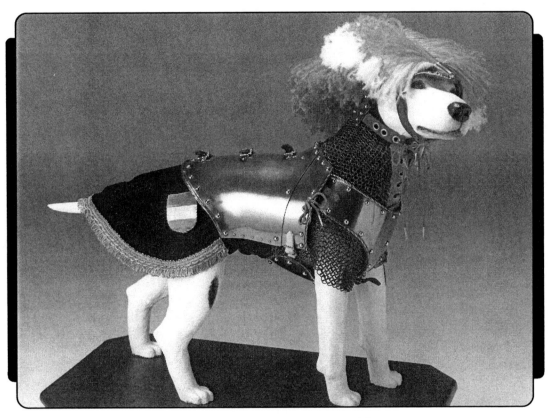

Helmutt of Higginswold
Higgins Armory Museum's Boarhound mascot
in his full 16th century style hunting armor

Golden Owl Publishing

Higgins Armory Museum

**Golden Owl
Publishing
Company**

Acknowledgements

Picture the Middle Ages

© 1994 Golden Owl Publishing Company, Inc.
P.O. Box 503, Amawalk, New York 10501
Phone: 914/962-6911 • Fax: 914/962-0034

Editorial Director & Graphics: Philip Wagner

Printed in U.S.A. All rights reserved.
Library of Congress Catalog Card Number 93-80805
ISBN 1-56696-025-8
Reprinted 1996

I wish to thank Ellen Kosmer Ph.D., of Worcester
State College, the medieval art historian who drew the
poster on which this book is based, and all the evocative
illustrations; Karen Hastie-Wilson who wrote the chapter
on Music and Dance; and the Massachusetts Cultural
Council as administered by the Worcester Arts Lottery
Commission, who funded an earlier version of this book.
I also want to thank the Board, Director and Staff of the
Higgins Armory Museum in Worcester, Massachusetts,
for their help and encouragement.

Linda Honan

Photo credits: Higgins Armory Museum - page 34b
Don Eaton - title page, 34, 74h

Picture the Middle Ages

Written by Linda Honan
Illustrated by Ellen Kosmer
Music and Dance by Karen Hastie-Wilson

Contents

	List of Reproducible Illustrations & Activities	page 3
	Clues to the Castle: How to Use this Book	5
Chapter One	Higginswold: A Picture of the Medieval World	7
Two	The Middle Ages: Historic Overview	9
Three	The Town: Craftsmen & Guilds	21
Four	The Castle: Lords, Ladies, Knights & Chivalry	27
Five	Heraldry & Coats of Arms	37
Six	The Monastery: Priests, Monks & Nuns	43
Seven	The Manor: Farming, Food & Feasting	51
Eight	Making Costumes & Armor	55
Nine	Music & Dance	65
Ten	Artists & Art	73
Eleven	Literature	81
Twelve	The Grand Finale: A Medieval Festival	89
Thirteen	Timeline & Vocabulary Activities	97
	People, Events & Reading Lists	98

About the Authors and Artist

Linda Honan

Linda Honan, the author of this book, grew up in the Irish countryside among castles and round towers. After studying and teaching medieval English language and literature at University College, Dublin (M.A. with Honors) and the University of London, she broadened her acquaintance with medieval art and culture through research trips throughout Europe, and in graduate studies at Yale University's Department of Medieval Studies (M.Phil.). As Program Director at the Higgins Armory Museum in Worcester, Massachusetts, she plans and implements programs for teachers and students of all ages. This curriculum developed from teachers' workshops held at the Museum, often in collaboration with other cultural organizations. Linda Honan has studied heraldry for many years; she gives frequent workshops for genealogists, and presented two television series on heraldry and Joan of Arc on Massachusetts Corporation for Educational Telecommunications' distance learning network.

Ellen Kosmer

Ellen Kosmer, the artist of the poster and illustrations on which this book is based, is a Massachusetts native whose love of art was cultivated through childhood museum visits and classes. After majoring in painting at Massachusetts College of Art, she developed her historical interests in graduate school, and was awarded a Ph.D. in medieval art history by Yale University. The author of numerous articles and encyclopedia entries on medieval art history, with a special interest in manuscript illumination, Ellen Kosmer is also a practicing printmaker whose wood-engravings have been included in a Smithsonian Institution traveling exhibition. Extensive travel in Europe, North Africa and India contribute to the rich medley of sources which helped create her medieval world poster, "Higginswold," for the Higgins Armory Museum, and the illustrations for this book. Ellen Kosmer is Professor of Art History at Worcester State College.

Karen Hastie-Wilson

Karen Hastie-Wilson, who wrote the chapter on music and dance in this book, has taught music at all levels, and has served as a music consultant, classroom music specialist and vocal director. She has developed study guides for operas as well as curriculum guides for schools and museums dealing with integrating the arts into diverse subject areas. Currently teaching in the Milford, Mass. Middle School, Hastie-Wilson serves as Artistic Director of the Pro Arte Children's Ensemble, a community children's chorus. She received her Bachelor of Music from the University of Massachusetts and her Master's from Clark University. Post-graduate work includes Orff-Schulwerk certification and studies at the Kodaly Music Training Institute.

Reproducible Illustrations & Activities

page

Title page *Helmutt* - Higgins Armory Museum mascot
Boarhound in hunting armor, 16th-century style

4 a Higginswold classroom poster

8 a-d The World of Higginswold - keyed plan

8 e Timeline of Middle Ages - foldout poster

16 a Europe and the Mediterranean - blank map

16 b Routes and Destinations, Merchant Trade Routes and Universities - map

16 c Routes and Destinations, Crusaders & Pilgrims - map

19 Word Search for Chapter Two

20 Merchants & Trades of the Town

21 Walled Town of Carcassonne, France

26 a Town Plan of Higginswold

26 b-c Guild Signs

26 d Typical Castle Plan

28 Bodiam Castle, England - 14th century

29 Saumur Castle, France - late 14th century

34 Tournament Armor - 16th C. German, on display at Higgins Armory Museum

34 a Helmets

34 b Armor for Field and Tilt for Graf Franz von Teuffenbach
by Stefan Rormoser, 1554, on display at Higgins Armory Museum

34 c Parts of Teuffenbach Armor

34 d Maze Activity

38 a Heraldic Charges

38 b Heraldic Shields and Crests

38 c Heraldry - Marks of Cadency

38 d Heraldry - Canting Arms

40 a Heraldry - Pennants & Tournament Tree

40 b How to Make a Banner

40 b How to Make a Shield

41 Word Search for Chapter Five

42 People and Possessions - Monastic Life

44 a Typical Monastery Plan

Illustrations & Activities continued . . .

Reproducible Illustrations & Activities

page

49	Word Search for Chapter Six
50	People and Possessions - On the Manor
52 a	People and Possessions - A Banquet in the Castle
54	Bayeux Tapestry designs
58 a-b	Costumes
60 a	Gown Pattern
60 b	Robe and Tunic Patterns
62 a	How to Make a Knight's Breastplate
62 b	How to Make a Knight's Helmet
64	The Minstrels' Gallery
67	Music - *Boar's Head Carol & Hymn to St. John*
70	Music - *Sumer Is Icumen In*
70 a-d	Music - *Washerwoman's Bransle, A Knight to Remember, Oats & Beans, Sarasponda*
74 a	Sutton Hoo Burial Metalwork
74 b	Viking Stone Cross
74 c	The Book of Kells - Decorated Initial "T"
74 d	The Book of Durrow - Decorations
74 e	The Book of Lindisfarne - Lion
74 f	Romanesque and Gothic Architectural Drawings
74 g	Flying Buttress
74 h	Statue of St. George - 15th C. German, on display at Higgins Armory Museum
76 a	Rose Window North Transept - Notre Dame, Paris
76 b	Stained Glass Tracery Patterns - Notre Dame, Paris
76 c	Gothic Alphabet in Goudy Text
76 d-e	Celtic Alphabet
76 f	Paper Bag and Box Castle Patterns
79	Word Search for Chapter Ten
96 a-b	Timeline & Vocabulary Activities
100	Famous Folks Activity
104	Word Search Answer Keys
106	Maze & Famous Folks Answer Keys

Clues to the Castle: How to Use this Book

This book is designed to provide all the information needed for upper elementary and middle school teachers to create a five to eight week unit on the Middle Ages. Homeschoolers can use this book just like regular classes; the final festivity might consist of a play and tournament.

For a longer or more in-depth project, supplement this book with one or more of the following Jackdaw and Golden Owl portfolios of historical documents: *The Black Death* and *Columbus and the Age of Explorers* (use with Chapter 3 of this book), *Alfred the Great* and *Magna Carta* (use with Chapter 4), *The Spanish Inquisition* (use with Chapter 6), *The Peasants' Revolt* (use with Chapter 7). Additional resources are suggested in the Reading List at the end of this book.

Unit Learning Objectives

Content Objectives

After completing this unit, students should be able to:

1. Explain when and where the Middle Ages occurred.
2. Describe the political and social systems of the Middle Ages; and discuss differences and similarities between life then and now.
3. Describe the homes, possessions and daily lives of people in each of the major social groups in the Middle Ages.
4. Discuss the achievements of medieval people in arts, inventions, travel and discoveries.

Skill Objectives

After completing this unit, students will have:

1. Developed critical thinking skills through learning, critiquing and comparing the beliefs and accepted theories of the Middle Ages with our own.
2. Developed artistic and linguistic skills through creating art work in a variety of media, and composing stories, poems and letters.
3. Practiced cooperative learning through the academic tournament, and/or the culminating feast, play or fair.
4. Expanded their understanding of other cultures through becoming familiar with a distant world's everyday life, social structures, learning and art.

Organization of this Book

Picture the Middle Ages is planned around the picture of medieval life depicted in the imaginary world of Higginswold, which is explained in **Chapter 1**. A poster of Higginswold is included; this can be photocopied, colored and displayed on the classroom bulletin board. Copies can be given to students for them to color, cut-and-paste, and use in making their own medieval pictures.

Chapter 2 is an overview of medieval history. This may be read by teachers at the start of the unit, and later by students who are filling in the timeline, writing reports or working on projects. It can also be used as a reference text as the unit progresses.

Chapters 3, 4, 6 and 7 are the heart of the book. Each of them deals with one of the four major social groups depicted in the poster: the craftsmen and merchants of the town; the nobles and their servants in the castle; the religious in the monastery; and the farmers and peasants on the manor.

Chapter 5 describes heraldry, a quintessentially medieval system of identification. **Chapter 8** has patterns for making simple medieval costumes and armor. **Chapters 9, 10 and 11** describe and give examples of medieval music, art and literature. **Chapter 12** explains how to put on a grand ending to the unit: a medieval tournament, play, feast or fair that can entertain the whole school, together with parents and friends. **Chapter 13** features both timeline and vocabulary activities, plus lists of famous persons and events discussed throughout this resource book, a reading list, and answer keys.

Sample Six-Week Unit

Week 1: Old World Exploration
Read Chapters 1 and 2. Using the Higginswold and timeline posters, begin the activity timeline. Complete some or all of the activities in Chapters 1 and 2. Read in Medieval Literature, Chapter 11, the sections on Caedmon, Medieval Language and Riddles, and work activities 11-1 and 11-2. Read about early medieval art and illuminated manuscripts in Chapter 10. Write your name in your favorite medieval script, and illuminate your initial. Add medieval names to the timeline activity, and words to the vocabulary column, "Middle Age Words". Send a letter inviting parents to help with the final activities as cooks, prop or costume makers, and characters at the feast. Ask the whole school to save fortune cookie fortunes (for the fair)!

Week 2: The Medieval Town
Read Chapter 3 and work the activities. Add new names to the timeline and new words to the vocabulary column. Read about Mystery Plays in Chapter 11, and work activities 11-3 and 11-4. If you plan to include a fair in the culminating activities, begin work on it now. Choose merchants and entertainers, then read Chapter 8 and assign workers to start making costumes and stalls, and gathering merchandise. Read Chapter 9 on medieval music and dance, and learn the *Washerwoman's Bransle*, a circle dance, and some old songs. Work activity 9-1. Assign students to be troubadours and musicians for the festival; work activity 9-2. Have a parents' meeting to work on the final events.

Week 3: Castle Capers
Read Chapters 4, 5 and 8. Each student designs a personal coat of arms and makes a pennant, shield or banner. These are then displayed along the classroom wall. The class chooses a motto, which is written in medieval script on a paper scroll (copied from the top of the Higginswold poster), and the best example is displayed. Read about medieval architecture in Chapter 10, and look at pictures of castles. Each student makes a bag or box castle (activities 10-1, 10-2). Look at a chess set and learn the moves. Discuss their relationship to medieval people and warfare. Read Chapter 12 and plan a life-size chess match for the finale. Draw your own playing cards with medieval people as the face cards. Read about Romances in Chapter 11, and work activity 11-7. If your finale will include a play, choose one of the students' adventure stories to dramatize. Cast it, start rehearsing, and work on costumes and props. Keep adding to the timeline and vocabulary! Read Music of the Castle and Dances of the Middle Ages. Learn a courtly line dance such as *L'Escargot*. Plan a tournament for the finale, and practice the four jousts in Chapter 12.

Week 4: Monastic Life
Read Chapter 6 and work the activities there. Make a mirror or gargoyle (activities 10-3, 10-4). Preachers used many stories from nature to catch the interest of their congregations. Read Fables in the Literature chapter, and work activities 11-5, 11-6. Read about stained glass in Chapter 10, and make one or more of the stained glass activities (10-7, 10-8, 10-9). Read Music of the Church, and work activity 9-4. Continue work on the timeline, vocabulary, play, fair, and feast. Have another parents' meeting!

Week 5: To the Manor Born
Read Chapter 7 and work the activities. Write in medieval script a chart of medieval foods, herbs and spices and display it on the wall. Work on the culminating activities. Prepare the room, finish costumes and props. Paint the life-size chess board on the ground, or mark out on a sheet for indoors. Meet with parents to ensure all is ready for the big event.

Week 6: Welcome to Higginswold!
Review all the material covered, and give students a test or quiz. Review the vocabulary and the timeline activity. Prepare all the artwork. Finish costumes and props. Call the most important collaborating parents to ensure none has emigrated. Pray for good weather, and have a wonderful Medieval Day!

Chapter One

Higginswold: A Picture of the Middle Ages

Higginswold is an imaginary medieval world created at the Higgins Armory Museum in Worcester, Massachusetts. It was designed and drawn by Ellen Kosmer Ph.D., a medieval art historian, in answer to a request for a picture of what you would have seen if you looked down from a high hill in fourteenth-century England.

As we look at the letter-keyed drawings on the next pages, we see a drawbridge (**A**) that crosses an encircling river and leads into the walled town (**B**) through a fortified gate defended by vigilant foot soldiers (**C**), servants of the noble lord who rules this land from his castle (**D**) some miles away at the top of the picture. The foot soldiers and their captain are garrisoned in a smaller castle inside the town (**E**), near the water gate (**F**) on the lower right.

Inside the town, narrow streets filled with people and animals lead into the cathedral square (**G**), dominated by the beautiful Gothic cathedral (**H**) on which the masons are still working. The craftsmen and merchants of the town tell the world their occupations by the signs (**J**) that hang in front of each house.

A knight (**K**) rides toward the town on the lower right, on his way to the lord's castle where he will offer his services as a "free lance". A merchant unloads barrels from a boat (**L**) at the town's busy water gate, and another boat bearing a dignified lady (**M**) approaches the town from the lower left, passing perilously close under the three-seat latrine (**N**) that overhangs the river. This scene is watched with interest by the Higgins Armory Museum's beloved mascot, the intrepid dog Helmutt (**O**), wearing the heraldic plumes and elaborate armor of an imperial boarhound.

In the top left corner, horses and cattle can be seen in the fields and pens around the manor house (**P**), which is enclosed by a high wall with a gatetower (**Q**). Inside the wall a miller toils at a windmill (**R**) that stands handily close by while another peasant guides a horse plow (**S**). The manor buildings are surrounded by farmland, both enclosed in fields, and open as commons.

Across the top of the picture we see a shepherdess with her flock (**T**), peasants making hay (**U**), and a lady and gentleman out hawking (**V**). In the top right, separated from these worldly activities by a forest and a pond, stands a monastery (**W**), with its church (**X**), chapter house (**Y**), and cloister garden (**Z**), inside a high protecting wall. Two monks or nuns walk a dog near their gates. High above the whole scene hovers an angel and dragon, symbols of the battle of good and evil fought by every person in this age of faith.

A Higginswold poster is enclosed with this book. This can be photocopied, colored and displayed in the classroom. Another copy should be cut into quarters, photocopied and enlarged for each student to use with the activities suggested throughout the book.

Activities & Vocabulary ➡

Activities

1-1. Buildings Then and Now. Identify the buildings in Higginswold, and write their names on one side of the board. On the other, write corresponding modern buildings. How did people live without shopping malls, factories, schools, theaters? Have students decide where they would live in Higginswold, and which of its buildings they would visit during a week.

1-2. People in Higginswold. Find and identify all the people in Higginswold. Who is missing? Name all the other people who might have lived in the town, castle, monastery and manor farm house.

Topics for Discussion

1-3. Career Choices. Most of the people in Higginswold live in the same house as their parents, or a similar house, and do the same kind of work. The blacksmith's son will be a blacksmith, the baker's daughter will be a baker. Despite its limitations, are there any good points in this system? (Continuity - security - parents helping children, and later in life, children helping parents.)

1-4. Medieval Social Groups. Divide the class into four groups, and assign each group to one of the following locations: the castle, the monastery, the town, and the manor farmhouse. Find the illustrations that show the people and possessions of each location. Have each group decide what people live in their location; what work they do; how they contribute to the rest of Higginswold society; and what they need from the rest of society. Have each group present its conclusions, and argue for the importance of their contribution.

Vocabulary Words for Chapter One

chapter house
cloister
commons (of land)
drawbridge
foot soldier
garrison, garrisoned
knight
lance
manor house
medieval
Middle Ages
monastery
monk
nun
peasant
walled town
water gate

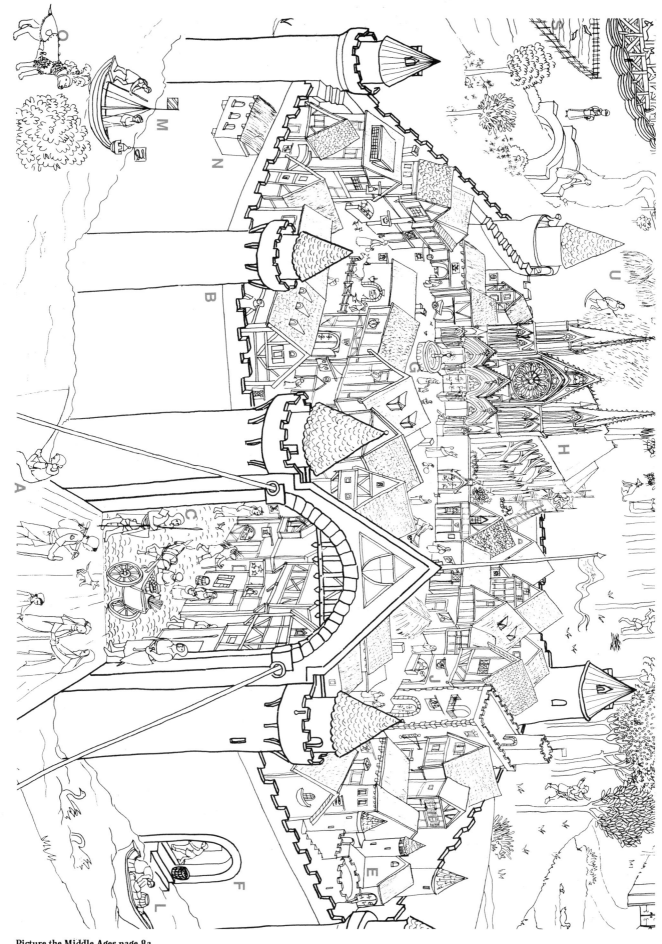

Picture the Middle Ages page 8a

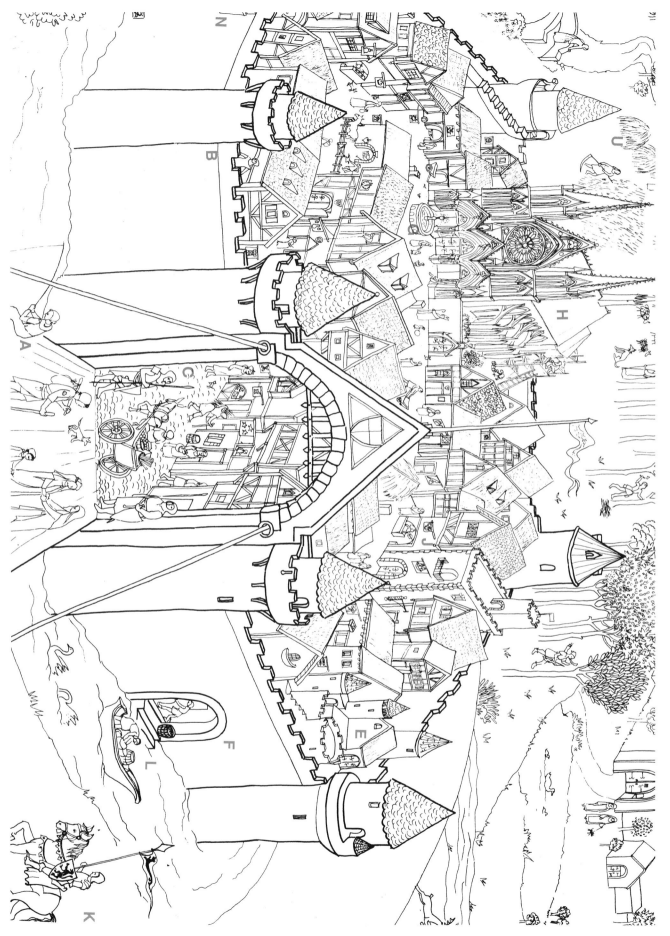

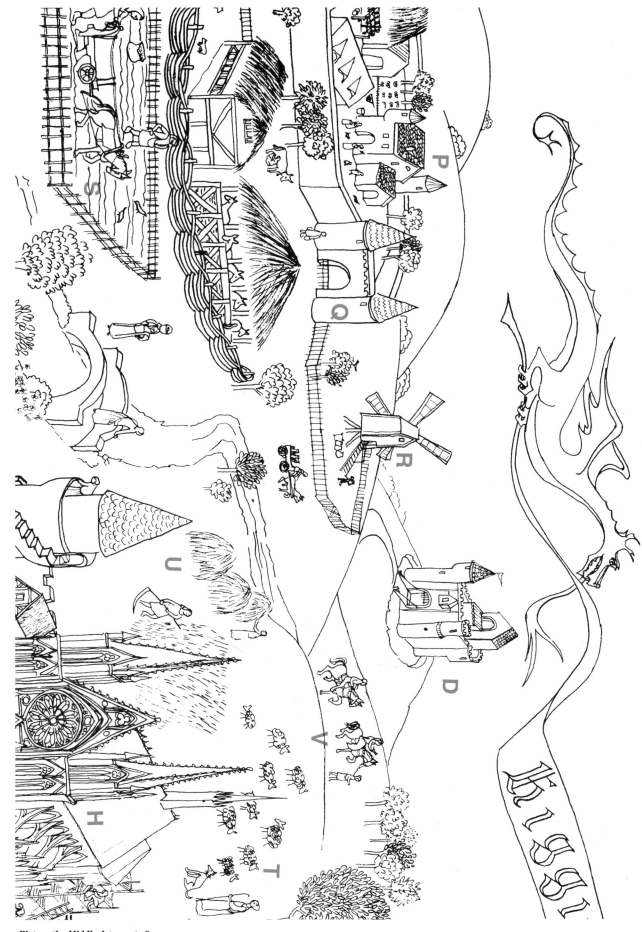

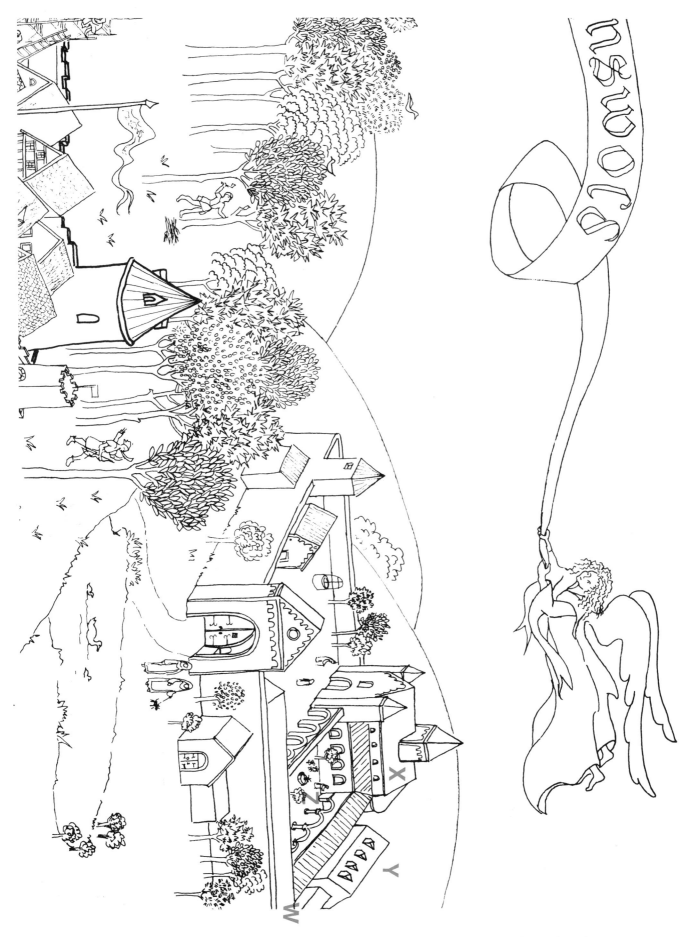

Chapter Two

Medieval Europe: Historic Overview

The Middle Ages is the name given to one thousand years of European history, from about A.D. 300 to about A.D. 1500. This period is called *medieval* from the Latin words *medius*, mid, and *aevum* age. (*Medieval* is pronounced med-ee-ee-val, not mid-evil — the word has nothing evil about it!) The Middle Ages means the period in the *middle* between the Roman Empire and our modern western world that began around A.D. 1500 with the *Renaissance* (pronounced ren-uh-sahnce), which means *rebirth*. *(Display and study the Middle Ages Timeline on the poster to the left.)*

The Early Middle Ages: 300-1000

The Roman Empire The Roman empire, with its highly-developed legal and political system, stretched all across Europe, the Near East and north Africa. The capitol city was Rome, but the empire included many other important cities. In 330 the Roman emperor Constantine the Great rebuilt the city of Byzantium, renaming it Constantinople and making it the capitol of the empire in place of Rome. Constantine legalized Christianity in 313, converted to it on his deathbed, and under him Christianity surpassed Mithraism in popularity to become the state religion. After Constantine's death in 337 the empire split into an eastern division with its capitol at Constantinople, and a western division with its capitol at Rome. The eastern or Byzantine (pronounced biz-an-teen) empire became the home of Orthodox christianity, while the western empire became the home of Roman Catholicism.

The Fall of the Roman Empire and "Dark Ages" In A.D. 476 the Goths, a Germanic tribe, deposed the last Roman emperor, and together with Vandals, Huns and other nomadic tribes, over-ran the old Roman cities. The empire's collapse was followed by several centuries of war and unrest, as nomadic northern tribes — Vandals, Huns, Visigoths and others — spread across southern and western Europe, gradually settling down and establishing stable kingdoms. This period was known in the nineteenth and early twentieth centuries as the Dark Ages, a term that referred as much to modern historians' ignorance of those times as to the quality of life then.

The Vikings Among the best-known nomadic Germanic tribes were the Vikings, also called Danes or Norsemen: seafaring Scandinavians whose skill at sailing and splendid boats enabled them to colonize Iceland, settle Greenland in A.D. 900, and probably reach the coast of North America, called *Vinland* by Leif Ericsson, who, according to accounts in the sagas, found grapes, wheat and trees in a fertile land west of Greenland, and thought by many to be New England.

In the eighth and ninth centuries, the Vikings were fearsome warriors dreaded by the neighboring peoples whom they repeatedly raided, looting monasteries and settlements. Over time, they became less belligerent, and some of them took to spending the winters in Britain, and gradually settled there permanently in small groups along the coast. They defeated or made treaties with local kings, became Christians, and founded many major cities, including Dublin and Limerick in Ireland (A.D. 840), and York in England. In France, the Vikings settled in Normandy, becoming known as Normans; from there, they conquered England in 1066, and gradually spread as far as Sicily. In Iceland, the Vikings established in the 9th century a stable society with democratic elements and a rich literary tradition of *sagas*, long prose stories, and poems. The sagas are still told today on Icelandic radio, with episode following episode day after day, listened to by huge numbers of people, like soap operas in our society.

The Age of Faith Medieval European society was profoundly religious. There was no freedom of choice or belief: anyone questioning the accepted religion of his people was condemned as a heretic, and executed by the state. The dominant religion was Christianity: western Europeans were Roman Catholics, owing allegiance to the Pope in Rome, and eastern Europeans were Orthodox Christians, owing allegiance to the Patriarch in Constantinople.

Spain was an exception: apart from the Christian kingdom of the Asturias along a small section of the northern coast, most of the country was ruled by Islamic Moors from North Africa throughout the Middle Ages, from 711 until 1212. Richly cultured, the Moors tolerated some religious diversity, allowing Jews to live in their land. There remained an Islamic kingdom in Spain until Ferdinand and Isabella reunited the country in 1492, when all Jews were also expelled from the country. Small numbers of Jews lived in other European countries, but their status was always uncertain and liable to restrictions. Diversity in the Christian community did not arise until Protestantism took hold in the Renaissance, inspired by Martin Luther (1483-1546).

The Monastic World The northern warriors who had defeated the Romans lacked their learning and civilization, and all the philosophy, literature and science of the ancient world would have perished except for one thing: the Christian church is a church of the Book, and its ministers must know how to read in order to carry out its services and pass on the knowledge of the Bible. Even in the darkest times, therefore, priests had to learn reading and writing.

Monasteries, religious communities of monks or nuns, were the only places in the early Middle Ages peaceful enough for the pursuit of knowledge. In the sixth, seventh and eighth centuries, monasteries thrived in the remote western and northern parts of Europe, Ireland and Scotland. In these quiet centers of learning, books containing the wisdom of ancient civilizations were preserved and painstakingly copied by hand.

The church's service books were written in Greek, in the Byzantine empire, and Latin, in the western Roman empire. All priests had to learn one of these languages, no matter what language they spoke in their homes, and so Latin became the language of learned people throughout all of western Europe. Since early medieval kings and lords could not read or write themselves, they employed priests to record their laws, figure their accounts, and write their letters: these bureaucratic *clerics* gave us our word *clerks*.

The Holy Roman Empire The nomadic northern tribesmen who had conquered the Romans gradually settled down and established kingdoms throughout Europe. The greatest of these kingdoms was that of Charlemagne (pronounced shar-luh-main), who was crowned emperor of the Western Roman Empire by the pope in A.D. 800. Charlemagne's capitol was at Aachen (pronounced ah-ken), also known as Aix-la-Chapelle (pronounced akes-la-shap-ell), in Germany. Charlemagne's successor, Otto I, would be crowned emperor of the Holy Roman Empire in 936, the largest political entity in Europe, stretching from Germany down to Rome.

Popes versus Emperors and Kings Throughout the Middle Ages the Holy Roman Emperor was the major political ruler in Europe, contesting his supreme authority with the Pope, as spiritual leader. Emperors and kings were believed to hold their authority by the will of God, whose representative, the pope, crowned them and confirmed their right to rule. Since popes were also secular rulers of lands in Italy in their own right, there was an obvious conflict of interest here. On the other hand, some important lords felt entitled to choose and confirm bishops as spiritual rulers within their lands.

The Investiture Controversy This ongoing conflict erupted in 1076 when Pope Gregory VII excommunicated Emperor Henry IV in a dispute over the emperor's right to appoint, or *invest*, the archbishop of Milan. Excommunication meant the emperor was no longer a member of the church, need not be obeyed by his subjects, and would go to hell if he died in that state. It was the popes' strongest card, which they played repeatedly in disputes with the powerful.

Penance at Canossa To show his repentance, in 1077 Henry went to Canossa, in north-central Italy, where the pope was staying. It was January, but Henry stood barefoot in the snow outside the pope's castle for three days until he was admitted and forgiven. Their reconciliation was temporary; soon Henry declared the pope an impostor, and appointed another pope; while Gregory declared no churchman need do any feudal homage to his overlord, a profound blow at the whole feudal system.

Feudalism The political system which sustained Charlemagne and his successors was *feudalism* (pronounced few-dal-ism). Feudalism was a system whereby land was held not by payment of a monetary rent, but in return for military or other service. Every landowner had a *liege lord* over him to whom he paid homage and owed loyal support, and a group of *vassals* beneath him, who in turn owed him support. A landowner leased land to a vassal in return for military service for a fixed length of time, often forty days per year. (Some vassals performed various kinds of domestic service rather than military. The *Butler* family served the English crown as butlers, for example, and the *Spencer* family were their *dispensers,* or paymasters.) In return, the landowner gave his vassal a piece of land on which to live, and supported him in any way necessary, such as in disputes with neighbors. The land given to a vassal was known as his *fief* (pronounced feef), which gives us our word *fee*.

At the top of the feudal tree was the emperor, who was no man's vassal; parts of his vast estates were given as fiefs to major lords: kings, dukes, earls and counts. These great lords in turn gave fiefs to lesser lords, barons and simple knights, who in their turn might have humbler knights, squires and freemen as their vassals. In this way, aristocrats were tied together in bonds of mutual support. Since several kings might be vassals of the emperor, their kingdoms were regarded as part of a single larger entity; the modern nation-state did not exist in the Middle Ages, when people felt tied to their lord, and their lord's lord, rather than to a particular nation.

All land-holders were part of this feudal system: vassals who could not perform military service, for example women and monks, had to hire replacements for themselves. *Free lance* knights, often aristocratic younger sons who would not inherit any of their fathers' lands, offered their services to any who needed them, in return for payment. (A *lance* is a long spear-like weapon.)

Medieval Society Medieval Society was static and conservative. Social positions were fixed at birth, and it was rare for anyone to join a profession or achieve a status other than his parents'. The lowest class was the serfs: farmhands who belonged to the manor on which they were born. They could never leave it, and their few rights under the law were determined by the customs of the manor on which they lived.

The most common way to achieve advancement was through joining the church, where talented young men of humble origins could be promoted to high administrative ranks as bishops, abbots or even cardinals. Skill at tournament and battle could also lead to advancement. Courageous and able young men were often knighted for their prowess.

Women had limited rights under the law, but practiced many different occupations, including medicine, textile production, writing and illuminating manuscripts, teaching, and farming. Women shared their husbands' responsibilities, overseeing their estates and farm workers, and had the whole task of organizing their households and supervising their children and servants.

The Later Middle Ages: 1000-1500

Magna Carta This *Great Charter* was a declaration of rights granted by King John of England in 1215 to his barons (lords) and the church. The barons united to force weak King John to sign this list of 63 clauses, which were understood to be a statement of the limitations of the royal power and the rights of all the kings' subjects to justice. The English constitution is partly based on this charter, which later generations believed to guarantee trial by jury and to prohibit taxation without representation.

The Crusades Beginning in 1095 and ending in 1291, the Crusades were a series of attempts to recapture Jerusalem for the Christian forces of Europe and make it safe for Christian pilgrims to travel there. Thousands of European knights left their homes and traveled to the east to engage the Islamic conquerors of Jerusalem. Their motives were unquestionably mixed: besides idealists who hoped to rescue Jerusalem and their own souls, there were landless younger sons hoping to acquire land along the way, adventurers hoping for adventure and the prospect of gain in foreign lands, and the bored or hopeless who welcomed any change.

Their battles had various outcomes, but were ultimately unsuccessful; the attempt to recapture Jerusalem was abandoned in 1291 when Acre, the last Christian fortress, fell to the Muslims. One enduring result of the Crusades was the fruitful encounter of curious Europeans with the rich learned Islamic culture, advanced in science and mathematics, and with its own extensive heritage of philosophy and literature. The name *crusades* is also applied to some later ventures of militant Christianity in other parts of the world, including attempts by the Teutonic Knights, a religious order of German knights, to spread Christianity among the Baltic peoples.

Children's Crusade The most tragic of the Crusades was the *Children's Crusade* of 1212, when a large group of children led by a French boy, Stephen, who was inspired by a vision, attempted to reach Jerusalem but either fell ill and died en route or were sold into slavery.

Knights Hospitalers During the Crusades some knights banded together in religious communities dedicated to liberating or protecting the holy places in Jerusalem, and to medical care for pilgrims. Orders of religious knights included the Templars (founded circa 1118), the Knights of St. John (founded 1113) and the Knights of Malta: the last two orders survive to this day, and operate charitable medical institutions in many countries.

The Black Death In 1334 an epidemic of bubonic plague broke out in Constantinople and quickly spread, carried by flies living on rats in ships. This plague is called the Black Death because it is characterized by black hemorrhages from the lymph nodes. Returning Crusaders brought it to

Europe in 1346, where as much as three quarters of the population died within the next ten years. In 1349 it killed one third of the population of England. This tragedy greatly enhanced the value of labor, elevating the demand for farm laborers and craftsmen alike, and hastening the change from the old tightknit feudal society to a new freer society based in towns.

Medieval Warfare Wars and battles large and small punctuate the Middle Ages. Lords constantly engaged in border disputes with their neighbors, and kings were for ever attempting to enlarge or protect their kingdoms' boundaries.

Hundred Years War Some wars lasted as long as the *Hundred Years War* between France and England, waged from 1337 to 1453 over the English claim to the French throne and their old provinces in France.

Wars of the Roses Hardly had this war ended than the English became embroiled in 1455 in a dynastic struggle for the kingship between the houses of York and Lancaster, whose badges were the white rose and the red, from which these wars are called the *Wars of the Roses*. They ended in 1485 with the victory of Henry Tudor over King Richard III at the Battle of Bosworth; he acceded to the throne as Henry VII, starting the Tudor dynasty.

The Growth of Towns When the Middle Ages began, the old Roman towns and cities were in ruins, sacked and looted by invading nomads. Early medieval society was rural, clustered around the castles of the ruling kings and lords. Monasteries were built in the countryside, and were essentially farmhouses, surrounded by the lands that supported them. Bishops, however, the church's regional administrators, established their cathedrals in the old towns of the Roman empire.

Life became more peaceful as the Middle Ages advanced, and travel increased, allowing merchants to cross the known world in search of goods to sell, bringing amber and fur from northern Russia down to Venice, where they traded with the spice merchants from Africa and silk merchants from Asia. Towns sprang up at crossroads and river crossings where fairs were held, and merchants gathered. With the growth of towns, the freedoms of townspeople increased, the beginning of a process that would gradually end the old feudal relationship with the local lord.

The Growth of Literacy As monasteries spread across Europe, some of the nobility sent their children to the monks and nuns for education. Literacy increased, and rich benefactors began to establish schools for poor children. In the twelfth and thirteenth centuries learning reached a level unmatched since the glorious days of ancient Greece and Rome: the first universities were established in several major cities — Bologna (1119), Paris (1150), Oxford (1167), Salamanca (1217), Lisbon (1290) — and thousands of students studied at them.

Universities were so called because they taught all subjects: theology, law and medicine were the major schools. Preparatory schools taught the *trivium* of rhetoric, logic and grammar — we still call elementary schools *grammar* schools! Secondary schools taught the *quadrivium*, music, astronomy, geometry and arithmetic. Together, the trivium and quadrivium constituted the *seven liberal arts*, a term remembered in our liberal arts colleges.

As literacy increased, so did the demand for books. At first produced only in monasteries, by the late Middle Ages the book trade was an important industry in towns, where highly specialized craftsmen wrote, illustrated and bound not only plain text books for students and clerics, but also highly-decorated and beautifully-bound books of prayers, poems and songs for lords and ladies who had acquired a taste for reading.

The Inquisition The words *Spanish Inquisition* bring to mind a terrifying system of unnamed informers, routine torture, and frequent public executions by fire, all in the name of religious conformity — to many people, the quintessential picture of the Middle Ages. In fact, the Spanish Inquisition was not established until the end of the Middle Ages, in 1478. The Inquisition as a bureaucratic system of eradicating heresy, however, had been established by the pope in southern France in 1233, and spread from there to Italy, Germany and, of course, Spain, where it was not formally ended until 1834.

Heresy, the acceptance of a religious belief, small or large, that was not in accordance with the received theology of the day, was regarded as a dangerous pollutant in the Middle Ages. If not checked, it could spread like an epidemic, so learned theologians were agreed that death by fire was the safest cure. Under the rules of the Inquisition, the land and goods of a heretic were seized by the local ruler, and sometimes shared with the local church authorities, so there were also material reasons for the long reign of this system of religious justice.

Joan of Arc A charge of heresy was also a useful way to nullify a political opponent. When the heroic French visionary *Joan of Arc* (1412?-1431), who had led an army against the English and brought about the crowning of the French king, was finally captured by her English enemies, they disposed of her by tricking her into an admission of heresy, which allowed them to execute her at the stake.

Medieval Science The generally conservative nature of medieval thought made experimental science unattractive to most scholars, but there were ongoing improvements and developments in scientific knowledge.

Agricultural Technology Agriculture was the main industry in the Middle Ages, and important innovations were brought about with the help of science. The ancient Greeks and Romans had harnessed horses with inefficient straps around their necks. As the horses pulled forward, these pressed on their windpipes, leading them to rear their heads in the attempt to breathe, as we see in ancient statues of horses and riders.

An improved harness, resting on the horse's shoulders and not his windpipe, was introduced into Europe in the ninth century, enabling horses to pull much heavier loads. Horseshoes were another important innovation, which allowed the use of horses on a greater variety of terrain. Horseshoes spread to western Europe from Asia in the eleventh century. An improved high-wheeled plow was also introduced in the eleventh century, which led to greatly increased production of crops.

Clocks Mechanical clocks revolutionized timekeeping when they were introduced in 1360. Before their invention, time was regulated on a daily basis by sunrise and sunset, which made for much longer days in summer than in winter. Those who wanted to sub-divide the daylight or night-time hours used hourglasses and water clocks. For most medieval people, time was marked by the sun and by church or monastery bells. The monastic day depended on sunlight, so it varied in length seasonally.

The mechanical clock changed that, marking out hours of equal length for every day in the year. Guildhalls and townhalls, the headquarters of the ruling bodies of independent cities, were quick to adopt the new regular time, and placed clocks on their buildings as soon as they were invented in the fourteenth century. This led to an important change in lifestyle, when the darkest winter day was decreed to be equally as long as the sunniest and warmest midsummer day. The old agricultural calendar which ordained many more hours of work in summer than winter was now overruled, and the hand-rung monastic bell was superseded by the new mechanical clocks of the town.

Medieval Scientists Among the best-known medieval scientists were two Englishmen. *Robert Grosseteste* (1175?-1253) was a Franciscan friar who taught at Oxford University and later became bishop of Lincoln. Grosseteste read Hebrew, Greek, Latin and French, and published studies in physics, mathematics and astronomy. His most famous pupil was *Roger Bacon* (1214?-1294?), another English Franciscan friar who studied alchemy and mathematics, and believed in the importance of controlled experiments.

Alchemy Alchemy was the great interest of medieval scientists: it was the quest to turn all base metals into gold, and to learn the secret of eternal youth. Alchemy was being practiced by the Arabs from the eighth century, and reached western Europe in the twelfth century, with the knowledge of ancient Greek texts that was being spread by scholars in the new universities. Alchemists concealed their research in a secret language, but their work in fact created the basis of modern chemistry.

The Medieval World *(See maps on next pages)* The medieval earth was fixed at the center of the universe, with the sun, moon and stars revolving around it. The modern concept of astronomy, in which the earth, planets and moon circle the sun, did not arise until the Renaissance, with the publication of the work of Nicholas Copernicus (1473-1543) in 1543, on his deathbed.

Europe occupied most of the medieval world map which centered on the Mediterranean. Jerusalem, because of its importance in the life of Christ, was often depicted as the central point in this map. Beyond Europe, the known world comprised North Africa and Asia Minor, with uncertain speculation about the nature and extent of the rest of Asia and Africa, until the great voyages of Prince Henry the Navigator's Portuguese ships in the fifteenth century. America was unknown.

The Vikings, brave seafarers, had sailed north to the Arctic circle and west to Greenland, and probably reached North America, without recognizing its vastness. In the thirteenth century the Venetian explorer Marco Polo (1254?-1324?) went to China, and returned bringing noodles, and telling of paper money, coal, and much else unknown to his native Italy, and with marvelous tales of the rich civilization of the East.

Travel and Travellers Despite the difficulty, medieval people traveled constantly, especially in the warmer months. The maps in this book show some of the most popular routes and destinations. Boats, propelled by oars or sails, were the preferred way to go: cheaper, safer, more comfortable and usually faster than land vehicles. Excellent roads had been built throughout their empire by the ancient Romans, but no one had built good roads since their Empire collapsed, and except where the Roman roads remained, land travel was difficult in the Middle Ages.

Mountains and hills had to be climbed, bridges were few and rivers had to be forded or crossed by ferry-boat. The land options were walking, or riding on horse, donkey or mule, or being carried in a wagon or on a litter (a hammock slung between two horses, often the choice of ladies). Travelers liked to travel in groups, for protection against marauders and for mutual entertainment, as in Chaucer's *Canterbury Tales*. Three to four miles an hour was a good speed for walkers, and since some people in any group would usually be on foot, this was a general rate for all journeys.

Merchants For merchants, travel was a way of life: their shop sign was often a ship. The more adventurous ones crossed large sections of the known world on a regular basis.

Circuit Courts Kings and great lords regularly moved their entire courts about their lands, packing up long trains of horses and baggage animals with their furniture and gear, and hundreds of followers. The court would move into several of the lord's castles in succession, demanding food from the local peasantry, distributing justice, and making a show of force designed to remind all the people of their lord's might. Having feasted luxuriously for a time, they would then move on, leaving the unfortunate peasants to eke out their scant rations until the next harvest.

Pilgrims Pilgrimages, the pious practice of visiting shrines connected with particular saints in order to pray to them in a favorable setting, were immensely popular with all classes of people, as we read in Chaucer. The assurance of doing good for your soul, and of satisfying vows that were often taken to bring about cures or other kinds of good fortune, together with the gratifying of human curiosity and the need for change and adventure, led to a spring-time thronging of the roads leading to popular shrines throughout Europe, and even to Jerusalem itself.

Students and Others Students traveled long distances to their universities; bishops and monks regularly visited Rome, to conduct business with their superiors; and during the Crusades, even children attempted the trek across the Mediterranean to the Holy Land.

Fifteenth Century Explorers Many great explorers expanded the known world in the fifteenth century. Prince Henry the Navigator of Portugal (1394-1460) sent as many as forty ships out around the west coast of Africa. Christopher Columbus (1451-1506) with his great voyages to the New World in 1492, 1493 and 1498, is the best known explorer of his age.

The End of the Middle Ages - The Emergence of Divergence In 1436, Johann Gutenberg (1397?-1468) of Mainz, Germany, invented the printing press with movable type - an invention which led to the end of the Middle Ages and the origins of the Renaissance. Thanks to Gutenberg, book production became vastly quicker and cheaper: now many people had access to printed texts, and ideas and information could be spread fast to huge numbers of people. In 1517, Martin Luther (1483-1546) posted 95 theses questioning religious authority and practice on a church door in Wittenberg, thus inaugurating the Reformation. Religious autonomy ended soon after with the rise of Protestantism. The idea of free speech, and freedom of reading and writing, began to take root; an innovation that would eventually supplant the medieval world of controlled information.

EUROPE AND THE MEDITERRANEAN

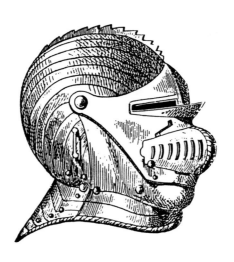

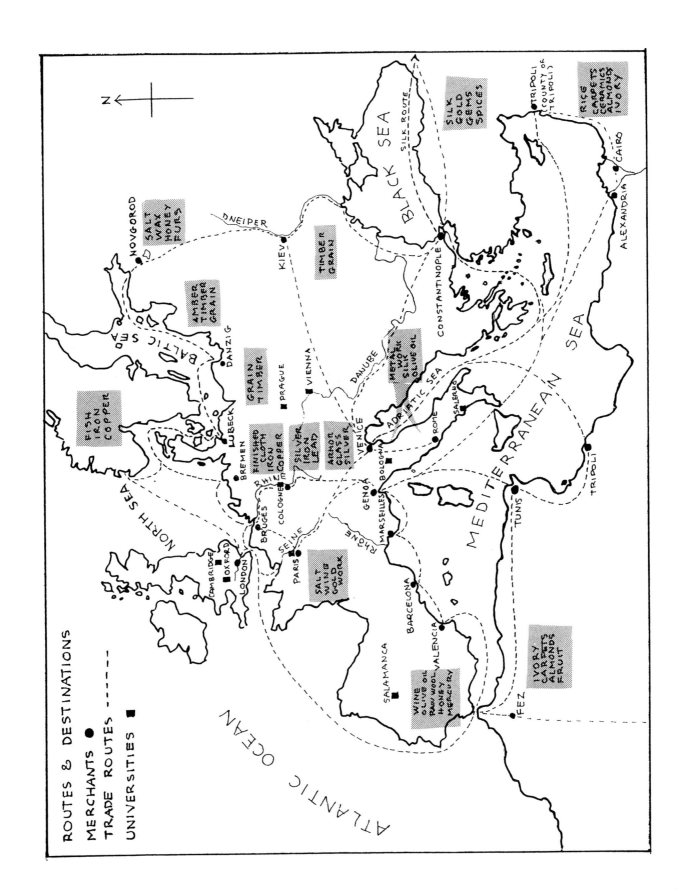

ROUTES & DESTINATIONS

MERCHANTS ●

TRADE ROUTES -----

UNIVERSITIES ■

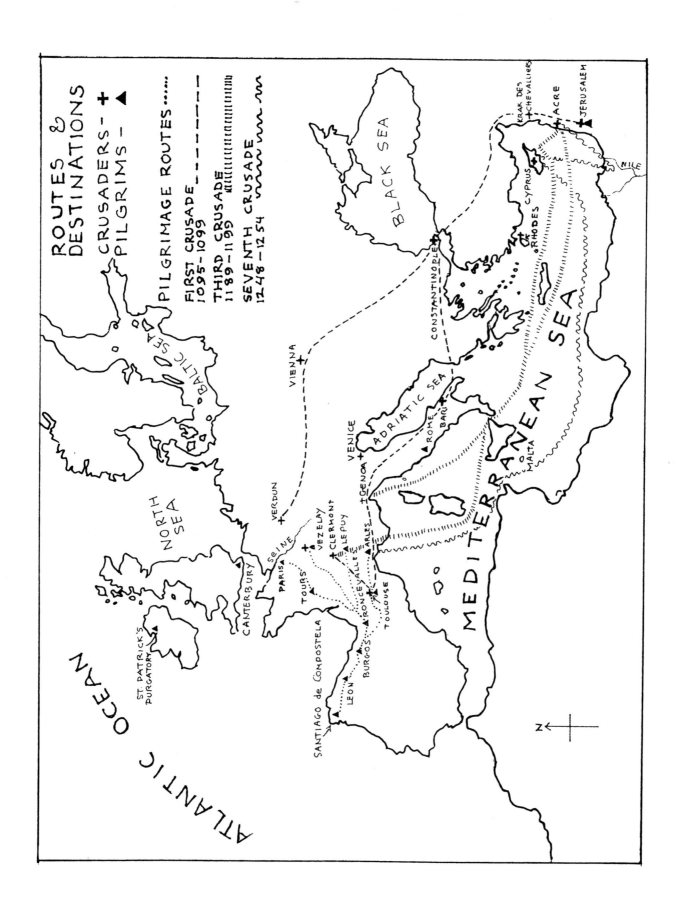

Activities

What's In A Name?

2-1. In the early Middle Ages, people had one name: John, Mary. This led to confusion, since many people had the same name. Several different ways of distinguishing between this Dorothy and that Dorothy came into use.

a. Adding the name of the place where the person lived: "Joseph of Boston," "Alice at Springfield." This was the standard way of naming kings, queens, lords and ladies, who were called by the name of the land they ruled: Elizabeth of England, Philip of Spain, Eleanor of Aquitaine, Richard of Gloucester. Some languages still use *of* before names: *de* (French), *van* (Dutch), *von* (German). Do you know any names that begin: De --------; Van --------; Von --------.

b. By adding the trade or craft that a person practiced: Thomas Smith (a smith is a metalworker), Alice Baxter (baxter means a woman baker), Paul Cooper (a cooper makes barrels), James Carter (a carter hauled goods on a cart).

Other languages use these kinds of names too: if your name is in a language other than English, try to find out what it means, and you may find it is a craftsman's name! These are the commonest kind of names, since most of us are descended from craftsmen. Name some real people with tradesmens' names. Other examples: Cook, Baker, Fletcher (a fletcher is an arrow-maker), Butcher, Carpenter.

c. Names can describe someone, and the nickname can then remain in their family. Native American names often include a descriptive name: Chief Wilma Mankiller of the Cherokee nation is named from an eighteenth-century ancestor. The Irish name Sullivan means One Eyed (*Suil Abhainn*, in Irish Gaelic). King Philip of France was called "the Fair." Vikings had descriptive names too, such as Harald Blue-Tooth. The poet Henry Wadsworth Longfellow must have had a tall person in his background! Do you know any people with descriptive names? Make up names for some famous people, or for people you know.

d. Some family names are the name of an ancestor's father: Michael Jack-son, Magic Johnson. The *patronymic*, or father's name, has become fossilized and passed down in the family. Other names that mean "son of" begin with *Bar* or *Ben* (Hebrew), *Fitz* (Norman French), *Mac* or *O* (Scottish or Irish Gaelic); names can end with *son* (English) or *sen* (Danish or Swedish). Complete as many of these names as you can: Bar -------, Ben -------, Fitz -------, Mac -------, O -------, -------sen, -------son.

In Russian names, the actual name of your father comes after the personal name and before the family name. For men, this patronymic ends *-vich*: Feodor Mikhailovich Dostoyevsky means Feodor son-of-Michael Dostoyevsky, for example; for women, the patronymic ends *-evna*. What would your name be in Russia?

Icelandic names use a *matronymic*. For example, Mary Smith's daughter Elizabeth would be called "Elizabeth Marys-dottir." What would your name be in Icelandic?

2-2. What would you like to be called? Would you rather have your mother's family name? Should we have another system of identifying ourselves, and indicating our family relationships?

2-3. Name all the medieval people you can think of, and add them to the activity timeline.

More Activities ➡

Trade and Travels

2-4. From twelfth century England, you are being sent with a cart-load of good wool cloth to trade. Where will you take it? What will you buy in return in order to make as much profit as possible?

2-5. Maps. Make two copies of the blank map here. Fill one in with important medieval places. Fill the other in with important modern places. Explain why some of the places are on both maps, and some are not. What made a town or region important in the Middle Ages, and today?

History

2-6. Write a story or play about the Investiture Controversy, the struggle between the pope and the emperor, and their meeting at Canossa.

Topic for Discussion

Freedom of Church and State

2-7. This important American principle was completely unknown in the Middle Ages. Are there any countries today where the state is subservient to the prevailing religion? Do you know any stories about life in such countries? Are there advantages to this system? Might it ever become the norm in the United States?

Feudalism and Democracy

2-8. Debate the good and bad points of these two systems. Japan also had a feudal society. How did feudalism arise? Might this system ever come back into use?

Vocabulary Words for Chapter Two

Black Death	Inquisition
Byzantine	invest (appoint a bishop)
cleric	knights hospitaler
crusades	liege lord
Dark Ages	Magna Carta
dynasty	Norsemen
excommunicate	pilgrim
feudalism	pilgrimage
fief	Renaissance
free lance	serf
friar (a monk whose mission is preaching outside his monastery)	tournament
	vassal
guild	Vikings
heretic	

Medieval Times Word Search

The words run forward, backward, up and down!

```
P   O   R   T   C   U   L   L   I   S
O   T   L   A   H   M   A   C   E   I
L   L   E   P   I   E   M   A   D   R
E   I   I   E   V   X   E   G   A   P
A   T   R   S   A   L   I   A   L   F
R   H   O   T   L   T   S   U   O   J
M   G   P   R   R   O   J   A   C   K
A   I   E   Y   Y   L   A   N   C   E
T   N   E   M   E   L   T   T   A   B
E   K   K   Y   L   A   D   U   E   F
```

Word List

accolade	.... blow on shoulder during knighting ceremony
battlement	.... gap-toothed top of castle wall
chivalry	.... ideals and institution of knighthood
dame	.... title for woman who is knighted
feudal	.... system of landholding by military service
flail	.... tool, later weapon, with wooden or metal head dangling from short staff
jack	.... leather coat reinforced with metal plates, whence *jacket*
joust	.... mock battle encounter between two knights
keep	.... central tower of castle
knight	.... lowest rank of aristocracy
lance	.... long spear-like weapon
mace	.... short club-like weapon
oriel	.... large window projecting from a bay
page	.... young boy being trained to courtly life
polearm	.... weapon whose handle is a long wooden staff
portcullis	.... iron grill that drops down over castle doorways
sir	.... title for a knight
tapestry	.... cloth hanging woven with a pictorial scene
tilt	.... wall separating two jousting knights

BAKER

DIVIDERS

LEVEL

COINS

Merchants & trades of the Town

MASON

PHYSICIAN

Chapter Three

The Town: Craftsmen & Guilds, Merchants and Travelers

Illustration: *Merchants and Trades of the Town* *(display and discuss illustration on lefthand page)* The big picture shows a *baxter*, a woman baker, selling to a customer. Loaves of bread fill her well-stocked shop. A pair of scales hangs over her counter, and the oven stands nearby. A cat rests on the counter, and a dog eats crumbs outside. Small shops like this, on the first floor of the craftsman's home, with a workshop at the rear, and a store-room upstairs, were the norm in medieval towns.

The small pictures show other trades - a mason and a woman physician, while some medieval coins, the nearly indispensable means of exchange, roll along the right border.

Medieval Towns Early medieval life was largely rural. Cottages of craftsmen and tradesmen clustered around the local castle, which offered protection against attack and employment in producing goods for the castle household.

Some Roman towns survived in ruins, and as time passed began to be inhabited again. The Catholic church, growing in organization and numbers, chose these old towns as local administrative headquarters.

WALLED TOWN OF CARCASSONNE — FRANCE

Cathedral Towns The church's administration was through a bureaucratic system of *bishoprics*, or *dioceses*, ruled by bishops who reported to the pope, the bishop of Rome. Bishoprics were established in the old towns that had been built throughout much of Europe as administrative centers for the Roman armies in the empire's heyday. The bishops' churches were named *cathedrals* from *cathedra* (pronounced cath-ay-dra), the bishop's throne, which was placed in his church. Thus the old Roman towns were rebuilt and revived as centers of church life and learning, acquiring schools and universities to train clerics and bureaucrats for the cathedrals.

Early medieval castles were largely self-sufficient, growing what food they needed, and using locally-made goods. As the Middle Ages advanced, life became safer, travel was easier, and the standard of living was improving. All this led to a greatly increased demand for goods, and a consequent rise in the craftsman's status, further enhanced by the decimation of the population in the *Black Death* in 1346-56. After it, craftsmen, and even peasant farmhands, found their services valued as never before.

For the medieval aristocracy, land was the primary source of riches and power, while money was much less important. But as towns developed, and merchants increased the range and variety of goods available, money became ever more necessary. Townsmen controlled much of the money supply, and found themselves in a position to bargain with their lords.

In the later Middle Ages, many towns obtained charters from the king or lord on whose land they stood, guaranteeing them many freedoms in exchange for tax payments, and freeing the lord from some of his feudal obligations to protect them. The *burghers* (townsmen) formed *trained bands* of militia to defend the town (as in New England), thus freeing themselves from reliance on their lord's men at arms.

Towns - Agents of Change In the late Middle Ages, the feudal aristocracy in their castles represented the old, and the towns, with their rich *guildhalls* (union halls) and *town halls* imitating the grandest dwellings of the day, represented the new. Magnificent guildhalls still stand in many European cities, testifying to the richness and power of the guilds. Civilization means *citification*, and the late Middle Ages saw a growth in the number of towns unknown since the fall of Rome.

Towns attracted the liveliest minds: students from all countries and all classes flocked to the new universities that were established in the twelfth and thirteenth centuries in Paris, Salamanca, Bologna, Oxford and Lisbon (see Chapter Two). The international nature of the student body was reflected in their lodging houses, where students from many nations lived with their fellow countrymen in houses named for their homeland: *Natio Francii*, for example. Runaway peasants flocked to towns, where even the humblest serf could find freedom: living in a free town for a year and a day automatically made a serf a free man or woman.

Craftsmen and Guilds Guilds, the forerunners of modern trade unions, became ever more powerful as the Middle Ages advanced, finally regulating every aspect of their trade, from training workers, to establishing standards, to pricing, to provisions for sick-pay and burial expenses. Members of a particular craft, say the *illuminators* who illustrated books, tended to live and work side by side in certain streets. Streets in some European towns are still named for the crafts that were practiced there in the Middle Ages: rue de Scribe, (Scribe's street) in Paris, for example, and London's Cheapsgate, (which means Merchants' Way - merchants were called *chapmen,* from the Old English word meaning to sell or bargain).

Master craftsmen lived upstairs in their houses, and worked and sold their products on the ground floor. A master craftsman usually employed one or more assistants, sometimes called *journeymen*, meaning laborers paid by the day, from the French *journee* (daily) *men.* The trained workers were helped by boys (and sometimes girls) who were *apprenticed* to the trade, lived in the master's household, and were bound to stay there for seven years, helping with all the rough work and learning all they could about their craft.

After seven years, the apprentice hoped to graduate as a trained member of the guild. Later, the young worker might try to become accepted as a master in his own right; for this he must make a model of the guild's product, sometimes in miniature, but always to a very high standard, in order to demonstrate his mastery of all aspects of his craft: these test pieces were known as *masterpieces,* and have always been prized as prime examples of workmanship. Guilds regulated their trades by elected officials, chief of whom was the *guild master,* who legislated all aspects affecting their trade. The guild masters, in turn, ruled the town as elected officials on the town council, headed by the mayor.

Women and Towns In general guilds promoted their members' welfare, but occasionally they were a detriment to workers. Women had particular reason to fear the rising importance of the guilds in the later Middle Ages, since guilds normally restricted membership to men, and as they gained in power they promoted legislation preventing women from practicing many professions formerly open to them, including medicine. An exception was made for the widows and daughters of guild masters: guilds often tacitly accepted the important contributions of these women by allowing them to become masters in their own right, running their workshops and training apprentices.

Taxes collected from members paid for the upkeep of guildhalls, and their sumptuous banquets. More importantly, they also supported sick or elderly members of the guild, and ran schools for their members' children. Some of these schools survive, and have become famous for the quality of the education they offer. They are no longer restricted to members of the founding guild, and offer a regular academic curriculum, not vocational training: in London, for example, the Merchant Tailors School is one of the most highly regarded in the city.

Merchants and Travelers Craftsmen normally lived and worked all their lives in their own town. Very different were the lives of merchants, who traveled constantly across all the known world, bringing goods from one area to sell in another, and returning with goods from afar to sell at home. Courage, initiative and many kinds of skill were needed by merchants, who had to cope with many different languages, and many kinds of currency, and must learn to survive bad weather, strange food, and bandits and pirates on road and sea.

Europeans had a great desire for silks from Asia and spices from Africa, and these were a staple of merchants; in return, they brought amber and fur from Russia and other northern countries, finely made swords, which were prized in India and Africa, and other regional crafts. Ports in southeast Europe, such as Venice, were great bazaars where merchants from all over the known world met to exchange goods and take ship.

Guild Signs *(See the illustrations and key to signs at end of chapter)* The craft master's house was home, store and workshop all in one. The family and apprentices lived at the back of the first floor and on the second floor; while the attic was often a store for raw materials, and most of the first floor was the workshop and retail store, open to the street. From the front of each house hung a *guild sign*, a pictorial emblem that told the passersby, who were mostly illiterate, what the master had for sale.

Guild signs were traditional, and to medieval people just as clear and unmistakable as the Golden Arches are to us. They often showed a typical object made by the craftsman: the goldsmith's rings and the armorer's helmet, for example. Sometimes they showed a tool used by the craftsman in his work: examples of this are the tailor's scissors and the blacksmith's anvil and hammer. Occasionally they referred to the particular name of the establishment: in *Higginswold*, the *Three Star Inn* is an example. Finally, we find a pun in the sun sign used by the illuminator, a playful reference to the two meanings of the Latin word *illuminare:* to shine, and to illustrate a manuscript (a handwritten book).

Townspeople One of the best remembered townsmen is Richard Whittington (1358-1423), a mercer (cloth merchant) who became Lord Mayor of London. The popular story tells how Dick was a poor orphaned kitchen boy, who owned nothing but a cat. His master, a rich merchant, was outfitting a ship to go overseas and trade goods. Wishing to become rich, Dick put his only possession, the cat, on the ship in hopes it would be traded for some treasure. Sure enough, it was bought for a fortune by the king of Morocco whose kingdom was overrun by rats and mice. As he waited for the ship to return, Dick decided to run away, but the ringing of the church bells of St. Mary at Bow seemed to say to him, "Turn again Whittington, Lord Mayor of London" — so Dick Whittington stayed in London and became rich and famous.

Activities

3-1. Why do the craftsmen in *Higginswold* have pictorial guild signs, not written signs? Identify and explain all the signs in *Higginswold*. (See illustration)

3-2. Draw a pictorial sign used by a modern business (McDonald's arches, Shell Oil shell, automobile hood ornaments, etc). Design a guild sign for one of these modern trades: computer programmer, florist, pilot, police officer, nurse or doctor, secretary.

3-3. How many of the craftspeople in *Higginswold* can be found at work today? Have you or your parents ever bought anything from one of them?

3-4. Did everybody in *Higginswold* shop at all these stores? Were some of these crafts made only for the rich lords and ladies in the castle, or the wealthier craftspeople? Which of these crafts were useful to the people on the farm? Or the people in the monastery?

3-5. Which of the *Higginswold* workers was the most important, or were they all essential?

3-6. Which one of these craftspeople would you like to have been? Write a story about yourself as one of them.

3-7. Look at the picture *Merchants and Trades of the Town*. Name the different tools and materials used in each craft. Make a list of the tools and materials used in these crafts today.

Topics for Discussion

3-8. Working within the home and outside. Medieval craftspeople worked at home: the master's house contained his home, his workshop and his store. The master, his wife and children all worked at the family craft. The same was true of farm families. With the Industrial Revolution of the nineteenth century, large numbers of people started working in factories, outside their homes. Compare life for the craftsman and his family in the Middle Ages, in the nineteenth century, and today. Is life today better or worse than in the past?

3-9. It is often said that twentieth-century women are untraditional because they work at a paid job. Is it true that women long ago did not work at a craft? Who took care of children in the Middle Ages? Was it wrong for children to work? Did children then spend time alone? At what age should children be allowed to work?

3-10. Now, at the end of the twentieth century, there is the beginning of a movement to working at home, as people form computer links with their colleagues. Will this be something new? What are the advantages and disadvantages of working at home?

3-11. Draw up a list of businesses and stores in your local mall or town. Compare it to the list on page 26. Which businesses are in your modern mall but not in Higginswold? And which businesses are missing from your modern list? How have our lives changed because of these differences?

Vocabulary Words for Chapter 3

apprentice
baxter
bishopric
burghers
cathedral
chapmen
diocese
guildhall
guild sign
illuminators
journeymen
masterpiece
militia

Key to Town Plan of Higginswold & Guild Signs

Illustrations on righthand pages: Houses with guild signs are indicated by an asterisk.
Unnumbered houses are small dwellings for workers in the town.
Drawings of the guild signs follow.

1. Armorer (with yard in front) *
2. Guildhall
3. Physician *
4. Cordwainer (shoemaker)
5. Tailor *
6. Apothecary (pharmacist) *
7. Inn *
8. Carpenter
9. Custom House
10. Castle
11. Tapestry Weaver *
12. Woodcarver *
13. Barber Surgeon *
14. Merchant *
15. Goldsmith *
16. Scribe *

17. Book Binder
18. Bone Carver *
19. Bishop's Palace
20. Glazier *
21. Cathedral (with fountain in front, enclosed garden, and school in back)
22. Cooper *
23. Blacksmith *
24. Illuminator *
25. Bakery *
26. Tavern & Inn *
27. Lawyer *
28. Banker
29. Mercer (cloth merchant)
30. Mason *
31. Town Walls and Towers

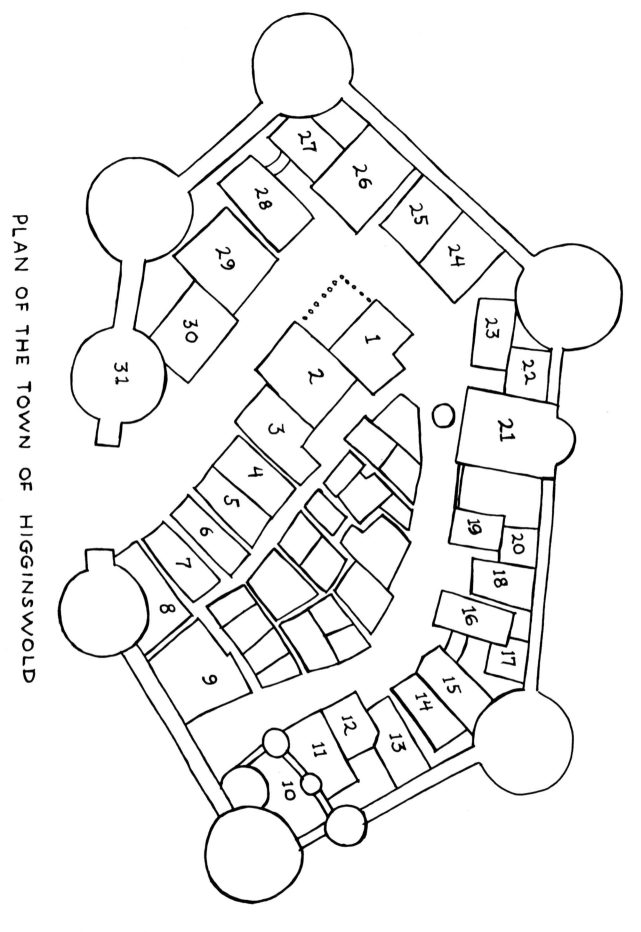

PLAN OF THE TOWN OF HIGGINSWOLD

GUILD SIGNS

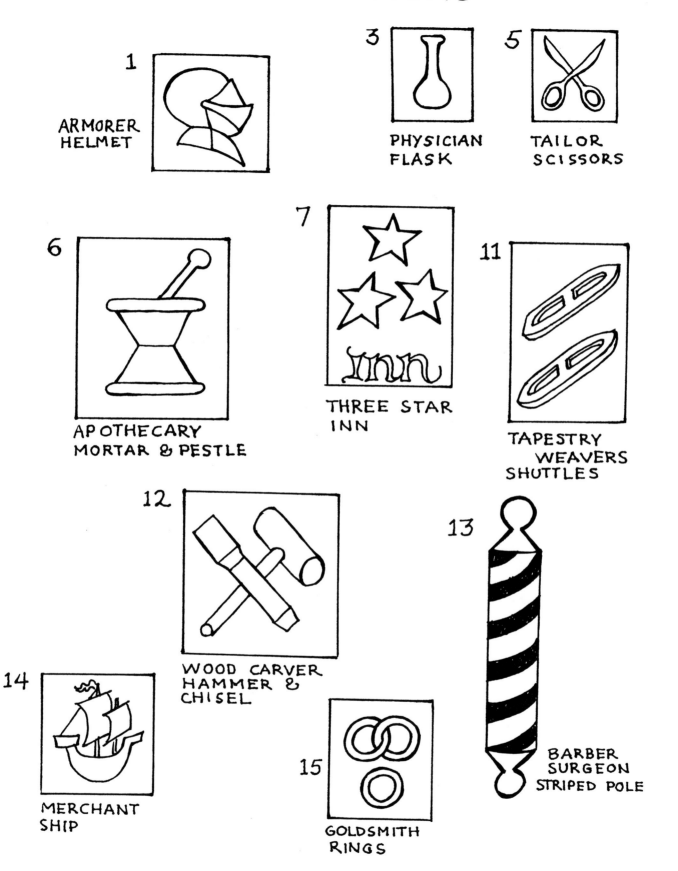

1 ARMORER HELMET

3 PHYSICIAN FLASK

5 TAILOR SCISSORS

6 APOTHECARY MORTAR & PESTLE

7 THREE STAR INN

11 TAPESTRY WEAVERS SHUTTLES

12 WOOD CARVER HAMMER & CHISEL

13 BARBER SURGEON STRIPED POLE

14 MERCHANT SHIP

15 GOLDSMITH RINGS

GUILD SIGNS

16
SCRIBE
QUILL & INK POT

18
CARVER OF
IVORY & HORN
STAG'S ANTLER

20
GLAZIER
TREFOIL WINDOW

22
COOPER
BARREL

23
BLACKSMITH
ANVIL & HAMMER

24
ILLUMINATOR
SUN

25
BAKERY
BASKET & BREAD

26
TAVERN & INN
BELL

27
LAWYER
SCROLL

30
MASON
TOWER

TYPICAL CASTLE PLAN

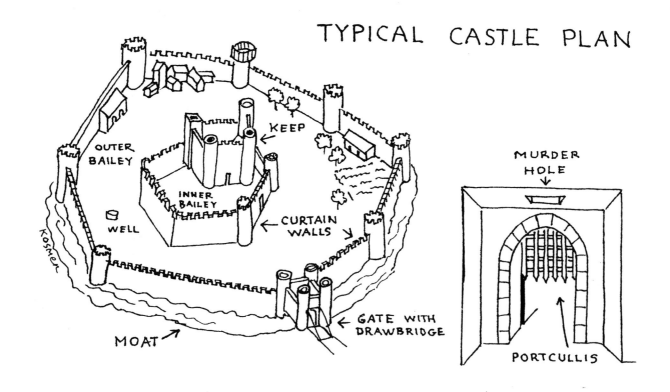

OUTER BAILEY

KEEP

INNER BAILEY

WELL

Kosmer

CURTAIN WALLS

MOAT

GATE WITH DRAWBRIDGE

MURDER HOLE

PORTCULLIS

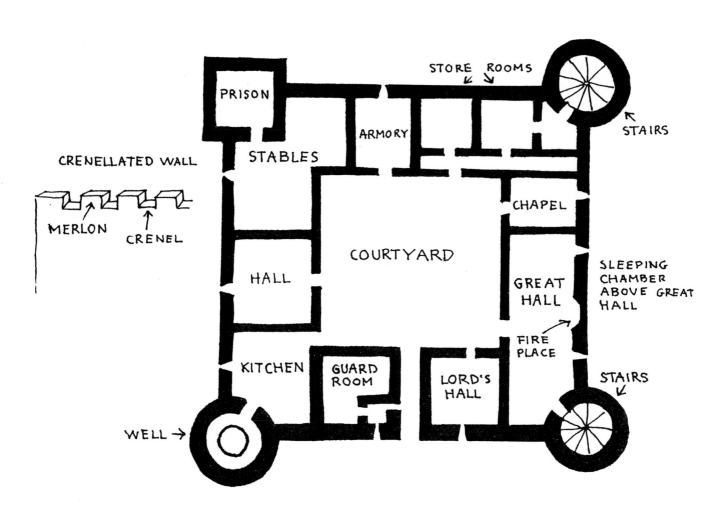

PRISON

STORE ROOMS

STAIRS

CRENELLATED WALL

ARMORY

STABLES

CHAPEL

MERLON

CRENEL

HALL

COURTYARD

GREAT HALL

SLEEPING CHAMBER ABOVE GREAT HALL

FIRE PLACE

KITCHEN

GUARD ROOM

LORD'S HALL

STAIRS

WELL →

Chapter Four

The Castle: Lords & Ladies, Knights & Chivalry

Typical Castle Plan *(Display and discuss illustration on lefthand page)*
The castle was home and fortress. It was home to the lord who owned it, and his family, and to his servants and men-at-arms and their families. The castle was also a fortress: it served to protect the lord's household, his knights and men-at-arms, and local peasants and townspeople in times of attack.

Castle design emphasized its defensive function. The earliest European castles were built of wood, and have all perished. But during most of the Middle Ages castles were built of stone, tall and strong, with few and small windows, and a door protected by a removable wooden ladder or a *drawbridge* with a metal grill called a *portcullis*. The heart of the castle was the *keep* or *donjon*: the central square (or sometimes round) tower that housed the inhabitants, which gives us our word *dungeon*, with the different meaning of an underground prison.

High towers allowed watchmen to see the approach of enemies from afar, and their gap-toothed *crenellations*, or *battlements*, protected an archer while allowing him to fire his bow from between the tall stone *merlons* around their parapets. Battlements often overhang the side walls so archers could fire their bows straight down at an enemy attempting to scale the walls, or pour down hot sand or refuse; this overhang is called a *machicolation*. Windows were also designed with bowmen in mind: narrow vertical slits (*arrow loops*) allowed an arrow to be fired out while protecting the inhabitants from attack by foe — or winter weather. *Murder holes* were cut in the floor over entrance ways, so that missiles or boiling liquids could be rained down on unwelcome visitors. Several sets of *curtain walls* protected the castle, enclosing the *inner* and *outer bailey*, or enclosure, from which we get our word *bailiwick*.

The location of a castle was crucial to its defense. Many castles were built on a cliff or mountain, high above potential attackers. Others border a navigable river, so transportation was easy, and drinking water in good supply. If all else failed, a ditch, or water-filled moat, could be dug around the castle. The excellence of castle architecture is attested by the large number that survive, despite the repeated attacks they have endured.

The Castle as Home: Chateau Saumur *(Display and discuss illustration on page 29)* With the passage of centuries and the easing of tensions between neighboring lords, many castles lost their importance as fortresses and were made more comfortable as homes. Larger *oriel* windows were cut into the walls of the *great hall,* the main living room of the castle, used for banquets, law courts, and all large gatherings. Tapestries were hung on the walls, and furniture became less perfunctory: tables were no longer trestles to be laid across saw-horses in the great hall by day, and taken down at night so the knights and men-at-arms could sleep on the floor. Castles grew larger, increasing the number of private chambers available for sleeping and retiring.

The Castle as Fortress: Bodiam Castle *(Display and discuss illustration on next page)* In the early Middle Ages castles were primarily fortresses, inhabited for only a few months of each year by their owners. Early medieval courts were nomadic, packing up and moving from castle to castle in a regular circuit across the lord's lands. They moved because of the necessity of showing the lord's might in all the corners of his estates; because only when he was in residence could the lord perform his function as judge and arbitrator in legal disputes; because the lord needed to keep in contact with his vassals and all his people; and because the court, with its hundreds of voracious mouths, frequently exhausted the food in an area in a couple of months.

ENGLAND
BODIAM CASTLE — 14TH CENTURY

Castles Today Castles still stand all over Europe; many are in ruins, but a large number are still habitable. Some are still lived in as private homes; others have been made into hotels; and some are open to the public as historic monuments that can be visited by tourists. Well-known castles that can be visited include Bunratty (Ireland), Neuschwanstein (Bavaria, Germany), the Tower of London and Windsor Castle (England), Caernarvon (Wales), the Palais de Justice (Paris, France) and Castel Sant'Angelo (Rome, Italy).

In North America, there are early castles in Quebec, Canada; San Juan, Puerto Rico; and St. Augustine, Florida. Some castles were also built in the nineteenth and twentieth centuries, as large homes for wealthy families, as national guard armories, and on college campuses. The Higgins Armory Museum in Worcester, Massachusetts has a castle's great hall tucked away inside a modern steel and glass building that is on the register of Historic Places.

Knighthood: Chivalric or Cavalier? The word *chivalry*, meaning the ideals and practice of knighthood, comes from the French word *cheval* (pronounced shuh-val), which means *horse*. *Cavalier* comes from the same root, but has come to mean boorish, ruthless and bold, the bad side of knighthood, while *chivalric* expresses qualities about the knight we continue to admire: courtesy, loyalty, gentleness and truth. These two words express the positive and negative aspects of knighthood as an institution.

The knight was, above all, a horseman. His horse was both transportation and an ally in battle: a well-trained war horse would kick and bite, and was rightly known as a *destrier* (pronounced des-tree-ay), from the French for "right hand." He was the knight's indispensable tool, as important as his sword or lance.

THE DUC DE BERRY'S
CASTLE AT SAUMUR — FRANCE   LATE 14ᵀᴴ CENTURY
DRAWING BASED ON THE TRÈS RICHES HEURES BY THE
LIMBOURG BROTHERS

From the simple bands of warriors who followed their lord into battle in the early Middle Ages, and from whom nothing was expected beyond courage and loyalty, knighthood evolved in the high Middle Ages, in the twelfth and thirteenth centuries, into a noble profession with high ideals. In the early Middle Ages knighthood was conferred by *dubbing* and *giving the accolade*, that is, by the lord tapping his vassal on the shoulder with a sword, embracing him, and bidding him be a true knight.

All through the Middle Ages, large numbers of men were elevated to knighthood on the battlefield, by their lords, in such a simple ceremony. Sometimes promising young men were elevated to knighthood at the beginning of a battle, to increase their courage and fervor. Sometimes their valor was rewarded at the end of a battle, when a victorious lord would repay his followers by knighting the bravest among them.

In the later Middle Ages, the knighting ceremony was elaborated and a religious vigil was created to prepare the knight-to-be for his new status. This ceremony required the knight-aspirant to spend a night at prayer in a church, before an altar on which rested his sword, symbolizing the offering of his strength and prowess to God. In the morning he took a bath to symbolize the washing away of his sins, donned a white tunic to symbolize purity, and recited prayers as his armor was placed on him. How many knights actually underwent this religious ceremony is unknown, but it was a popular topic in medieval literature.

Knights, Squires and Pages No one was born a knight: even the sons of kings and emperors had to earn the honor, although for them it was a certainty that they would become knights at some time in their early manhood. Training for knighthood began for aristocratic boys in early childhood. At age eight, a noble boy was sent away from home to the household of a friend or relative, where he became a *page* in the service of the lady of the castle. She taught him courtesy, table manners, which included carving and serving, and polite speech and decorum; while clerical tutors taught him reading and writing, religious knowledge and music, and more advanced learning if the household were particularly cultured.

At age fourteen, the page was handed over to the lord of the castle, to be trained as a *squire*. The squire's duties were intended to teach him all the practical knowledge he would need as a knight. He spent his time in service to a knight in the household. He learned horsemanship, and the care of horses. He learned how to use sword and lance, and all the other weapons of his age. He helped his master in and out of his armor, and helped polish and mend it after each wearing, polishing it with a mixture of grease and sand, before wrapping each piece carefully in cloth. If all went well, in about five years, at age nineteen or so, the squire was ready for knighthood, and returned to his home to assume adult duties. In an age without standing national armies, the knight's military service was vital to the defense of his homeland. The Middle Ages also lacked a police force, and the knight could find himself called on to enforce the peace in his lord's name.

Famous Knights In Britain, the most famous knights were King Arthur and his knights of the Round Table, and St. George the Dragon Slayer, who became Patron Saint of England. In our own day, British people who achieve success in their profession may be knighted by the monarch. When that happens, a man is addressed as *Sir* and a woman as *Dame*. Some current examples are Dame Kiri Te Kanawa, the New Zealand opera singer, and Sir Lawrence Olivier, the actor. The higher rank of baron may also be conferred, and those so honored are addressed as Lord or Lady: Margaret Thatcher is now Lady Thatcher, and Sir Lawrence ended his life with the higher rank, becoming Lord Olivier.

King Arthur and the Knights of the Round Table Modern research suggests Arthur was probably a British chieftain, or minor king, living in the troubled sixth century, when the Anglo-Saxons were settling Britain from their home in Frisia (modern Belgium), and medieval Britain was evolving from the old Roman colony. Place names and literature associate Arthur with Wales and southern England, from Winchester to Cornwall, as well as with Ireland: which places him in the southwestern range of the areas settled by the Celts — Wales, Ireland and Scotland.

Arthur's fame grew and spread throughout medieval Europe, and poets and troubadours wrote about him in many different languages. The most famous English telling of his story was the *Morte d'Arthur*, or *Death of Arthur*, written by Sir Thomas Malory, who died in 1471. Malory's prose tale is a long, engrossing account of the adventures of Arthur and his knights.

Arthur, whose father was the Welsh king Uther Pendragon, became famous for establishing law and order in his kingdom, and for gathering knights from far and wide to be part of his fellowship, the Knights of the Round Table, a group renowned for high standards of honesty, law enforcement and charitable help for the weak and needy. His famous castle was called Camelot (possibly at Cadbury, in southern England), and his wondrous sword was called Excalibur. The peace he established ended when his beloved wife Queen Guinevere fell in love with his favorite knight Sir Lancelot du Lac, breaking the solidarity of the Knights of the Round Table.

According to legend, he did not die, but when mortally wounded, was taken away by fairy women to the isle of Avalon, a magical Celtic Land of Youth from where he will return when his country most needs him; his supposed tomb bears the legend, *Hic jacet Arthurus, rex quondam et futurum* - 'Here lies Arthur, the once and future King'. According to some versions of the story, he was killed by Mordred, his son by an incestuous liaison with his magical half sister Morgana la Fee. (See Chapter Ten)

St. George the Dragon Slayer Although patron saint of England, St. George was probably a soldier who defended Christianity in the near east in the fourth century. His story was elaborated into a heroic tale of slaying a dragon and defending his people, or sometimes a hapless princess. His banner was a red cross on a white field, which became the basis of the British Union Jack flag. Medieval art often shows him actually stabbing the dragon; he was also a popular subject for medieval plays. See the photograph of a fifteenth-century statue of St. George in this book.

Knightly Sports Knights and squires spent much of their time, when not actually in battle, preparing for it. Two of their most popular amusements, hunting and jousting in tournaments, were directly related to warfare, and used similar horsemanship and weaponry. *Hunting*, a passion with the aristocracy, was a test of horsemanship and courage. Its basic function of providing much needed fresh meat to enhance a very limited diet was equaled in importance by its role as a sport that offered ample opportunity for displays of courage and prowess, and for elegant dress, ritual and equipment.

The Tournament The *tournament*, the great sporting combat enjoyed by all medieval aristocrats, was a mock battle that sometimes erupted into the real thing. Tournaments were held from the twelfth century on; although most had died out by the eighteenth century, there were still some being held in our own century. The tournament consisted of a series of *jousts* or *melees,* and usually lasted a week or more. Jousts were individual matches between a pair of knights, and were usually conducted by the rules; but the *melee*, a team sport in which one side battled with another, often got out of hand. Tournaments were held by kings and great lords, and were planned months or even years in advance, with *heralds*, messengers of the king or lord, riding far and wide to proclaim the tournament and invite noble knights to participate.

Tournaments were held to celebrate weddings and coronations, and were usually limited to nobly-born competitors. The city of Nuremberg in Germany was exceptional in holding tournaments called "bachelor jousts" for craftsmen and merchants of the city. Women did not usually compete in jousts, although the famous Queen Eleanor of Aquitaine was said to joust with her ladies, wearing golden spurs.

Knights would travel hundreds of miles to take part in a tournament, and spend large sums of money on appropriate armor and weapons for the particular kinds of joust which the host had chosen. Tournaments had strict rules, and there was a great deal of variety in the armor and weapons used. Jousts could be fought on foot, with swords, like modern fencing, or a variety of other weapons; or they could be fought on horseback, with lances, long spear-like weapons whose tips could be either blunt or pointed, single or multi-pronged. Axes and maces were also used.

The aim of the tournament was not to kill your opponent, but to win glory and prizes by defeating him. Strict rules were observed as to where you could hit your opponent and what kind of weapons you could use. Nevertheless, jousting was a very dangerous sport, and participants were sometimes maimed and even killed. Attempts were made to make tournaments safer, by the use of very heavy specialized armor, that could weigh over one hundred pounds; and by the use of the *tilt*, a six-foot high wall between contestants jousting with lances on horseback. The tilt prevented the horses from colliding, and forced the jousters to aim their lances across their horses' necks at an angle that lessened the force of the blow.

A Day at the Tournament Gaily patterned tents dotted the field where the tournament would be held, each decorated with the heraldic colors of the participants. Stands were erected for the noble ladies and older men who would be onlookers, while local peasants and townsfolk crowded around the barriers where the knights would compete. A *tilt* might have been erected in the *lists* — the field of competition.

Music was an important part of the tournament, and trumpeters and other musicians were ready for the signal to start. The lord who was hosting the tournament might designate a *tournament tree*, on which knights hung their gaily-painted shields to indicate their intention of competing. Heralds regulated admission to the tournament, identifying unknown entrants from their coats of arms, and dismissing those whose birth was ignoble. Ladies were sometimes the final arbiters, rejecting any knights who had acted discourteously.

Once the signal was given to start the jousts, the competing knights, gorgeous in their tournament finery, were led on to the field. Their ladies, who might wear gowns to match their lords' coats of arms, would give them a favor to wear, often a silk scarf tied on the arm: whence our expression, to *wear your heart on your sleeve*. The knights' squires would help them onto their horses, fasten on their helmets, hand them their lance or other weapon, and the tournament would begin.

After an afternoon of jousting, there might be a competition to choose a *Queen of Beauty* among the ladies in the stands. Then everyone would return to the host's castle for an evening of feasting and entertainment. This would be continued every day for seven to fourteen days, and then everyone would return home, with those who had been victorious in the jousts considerably richer.

Knightly Gear One of the great attractions of winning a tournament was the value of the prize, often including your opponent's armor and horse, which the loser usually bought back. To protect well, and at the same time allow the knight to move freely, armor had to fit perfectly, and well-to-do people had theirs custom-made. Someone else's armor was not particularly useful, unless by chance you happened to be the same size. If a knight gained much weight, he had to order new armor!

Who Wore Armor Poor foot soldiers, craftsmen and peasants following their master to battle, had little armor, and certainly nothing custom-made. An old helmet, and perhaps a *jack*, a reinforced leather coat, was all they could expect. Their weapons were designed to reach up to the knight on horseback: *polearms*, sturdy long wooden-hafted pikes and halberds, were able to overcome the height advantage of the mounted knight, and might find the *chink in his armor*. Women sometimes conducted sieges in defense of their property, as the Scottish Countess of Buchan did in the four-teenth century, and the English gentlewoman Margaret Paston did in the fifteenth century, but they rarely wore armor or took part in combat. The great exception is the French saint Joan of Arc (1412?-31), the indomitable teenager who defeated the English army in 1429 and saw her prince crowned king of France. A suit of armor was made for her by command of the prince. Her life ended disastrously: accused of heresy, she was burned at the stake by the English.

Evolution of Armor - *Mail* Until about 1250, the best armor available to the medieval knight was made of *mail*, a flexible material made of iron rings linked together. (The word comes from the French word, *maille*, which means a net.) Mail could be used to cover the entire body: a mail coat called a *hauberk*, mail leggings called *chausses* (pronounced show-ss), mail gauntlets and a mail head covering called a *coif*. Although it offered good mobility to the knight, and protected well against slashing weapons such as the sword and even piercing weapons such as spears and arrows (which rarely penetrated more than a fraction of an inch, and stuck in the padded lining worn under the armor), mail had one major defect — it did not protect well against crushing weapons such as the *mace*, a club with an iron head, or *flail*, a club with an iron head swinging from a chain.

Transitional Armor To protect against these, the knight carried a shield, but by 1250 the armorers began to attach solid plates to the mail armor, creating what is called *transitional armor*. With a solid iron helmet, and solid plates on vulnerable parts such as the knees, shoulders, and chest, the knight was better protected.

Plate Armor *(see illustrations of helmets and Teuffenbach armor on next pages)* By 1400 the armorers were able to cover virtually the entire body in solid iron and steel plate, and the age of *plate armor* had begun. Beautiful suits of overlapping plates of iron and steel, shaped both to deflect weapons and to mimic fashionable clothing, ornamented with etched patterns, colors and even gold, the armors of the fifteenth and sixteenth centuries are works of the highest craftsmanship, combining great technical ingenuity and artistic achievement.

Combat Armor Knights who could afford it owned specialized armor for various purposes. The three major types of armor were combat armor, ceremonial armor, and tournament armor. *Combat armor* was flexible, suitable for use with a variety of weapons, allowed the knight consider-able mobility, and usually weighed about sixty pounds. All of its surfaces are designed to deflect weapons away from vital areas of the body — the heart, the neck. Wearing his armor, the knight had to be able to mount and dismount his horse without help on the battlefield, although in happier circumstances his squire would help him on and off, possibly with a mounting block (a short set of movable wooden steps). There is no evidence that cranes were ever used to lower knights on to their horses!

Ceremonial Armor *Ceremonial armor*, worn for parades and ceremonies at court, is extremely lightweight, averaging thirty pounds, and is often covered with heavy decorative embossed patterns in which a weapon could stick. Ceremonial armor has virtually no defensive value.

Tournament Armor *Tournament armor* was heavy, extremely protective, designed to be used with a limited range of weapons, and offered the knight limited mobility. The weight of tournament armor averages eighty pounds and can exceed one hundred, slowing the knight down and tiring him, but offering excellent protection. The helmet in a tournament armor is often attached to the breastplate and backplate so the wearer cannot turn his head. In a joust against a single opponent who is charging straight at you from the front, it is not important to be able to turn your head, and having your neck held in a vice lessens the likelihood of breaking it if you fall off your horse.

Horse Bard *(See below)* Besides armor for himself, the knight had armor for his horse, known as *bard*, which often matched his own in design. In the late Middle Ages and Renaissance, horses were commonly given a helmet called a *shaffron*, and a breastplate called a *peytral*. A horse had to be sturdily built to bear the weight of an armored man as well as his own armor. The medieval warhorse breed, the *destrier*, resembles the modern hunter or Lippizaner stallion, with a powerful stocky body but slender legs. These horses were part of their master's fighting team, and were trained to bite and kick.

Castle Games Besides chess (see Chapter 11), another board game popular in the Middle Ages was checkers, which was called the *Jeu des Dames* (pronounced zhuh-day-dam), which means *The Ladies' Game*. Games played with knuckle-bones, such as Fives, were also popular. Dice evolved from knuckle-bones, which had been used as game pieces from ancient Greek and Roman times. Dice were made of bone or wood, and were marked similarly to modern dice. Backgammon was known from the tenth century. Blindman's Buff and Nine-men's morris were popular medieval games for adults and children.

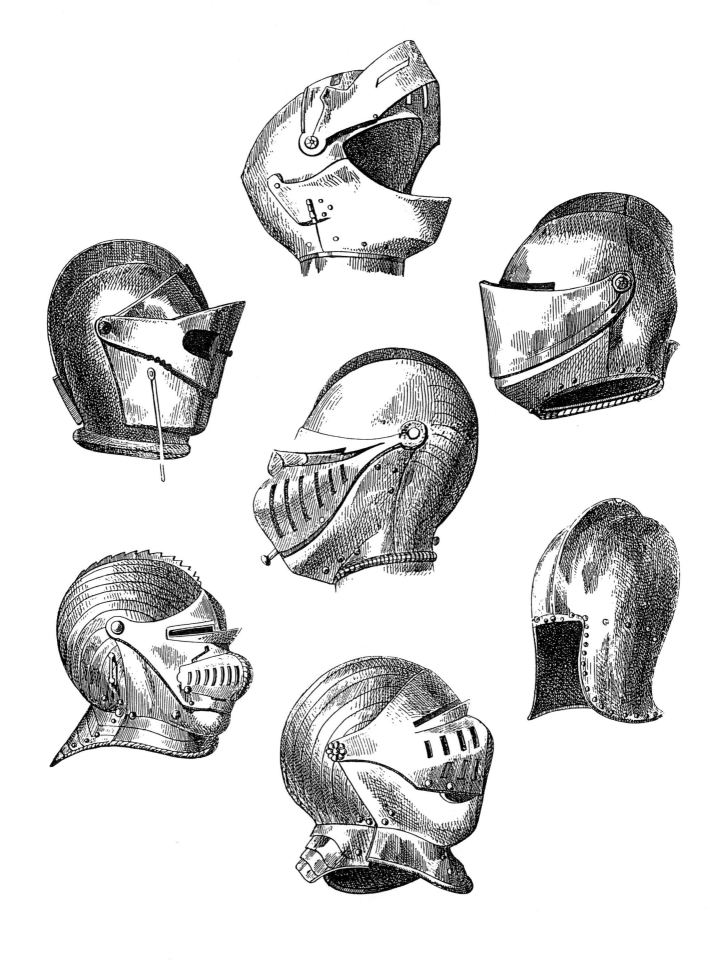

PLATE ARMOR FOR COMBAT & TOURNAMENT

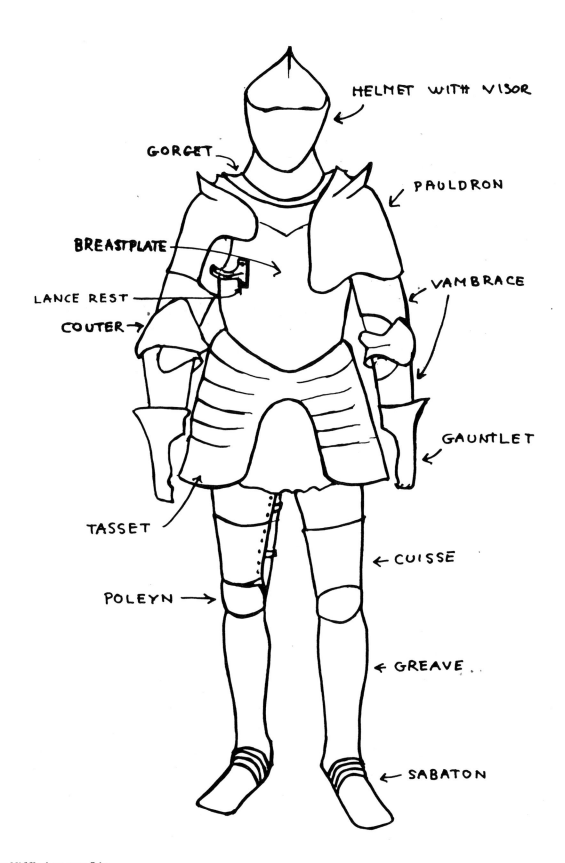

HELMET WITH VISOR

GORGET

PAULDRON

BREASTPLATE

LANCE REST

COUTER →

VAMBRACE

GAUNTLET

TASSET

CUISSE

POLEYN →

GREAVE

SABATON

Picture the Middle Ages page 34c

Can you guide Sir Lancelot through the maze to his castle?

Activities

See the heraldic and armor-making activities following Chapters 5 and 8, and the castles to design in activities 10-1 and 10-2.

4-1. Card games were popular in the fifteenth century; painted and printed playing cards survive from that time. Draw a set of playing cards using Arthurian characters as the face cards.

4-2. Topic for discussion: medieval kings and queens, lords and ladies, inherited their positions. Is this a good system for ruling a country? Why did this system last so long, and exist in so many countries? Write down all the reasons you can think of that make monarchy a good way to rule, and all the reasons that make it bad. Debate monarchy versus democracy.

4-3. Learn one or more of the old games discussed above. Impersonate medieval people, perhaps a group of knights and ladies from Camelot, and play these games.

4-4. Mazes were popular in medieval gardens, and were sometimes designed on church floors to remind visitors how hard it is to find the straight path to heaven. *(Solve the maze on the lefthand page.)*

VocabularyWords for Chapter Four

accolade	joust
bachelor joust	keep
backplate	knight
bailey	lance
bailiwick	mace
bard	machicolation
battlement	melee
breastplate	merlon
chausses	murder hole
chivalry	oriel
coif	page
crenellation	peytral
dame	plate armor
destrier	polearm
donjon (tower)	portcullis
dungeon (underground prison)	shaffron
flail	sir
gauntlet	squire
great hall	tapestry
halberd	tilt
hauberk	tournament
herald	tournament tree
jack	transitional armor

Chapter Five

Heraldry and Coats of Arms

Heraldry and Coats of Arms *(Display and discuss the illustrations on the next pages)* Heraldry is the name given to the system of identification used by medieval knights, who painted a design on their shields by which they could be known. The earliest examples of heraldry date from the twelfth century, which was also the time when knights began to wear a new kind of helmet that completely covered their faces, the *barrel helm* or *great helm*, which looks like an upturned iron bucket with a small eye slit. The earliest coat of arms we can find today is on the funeral enamel portrait of Count Geoffrey of Anjou, known as Geoffrey Plantagenet, founder of the English Plantagenet dynasty. Geoffrey died in 1151, and his tomb in Le Mans Cathedral shows him holding a shield with lions *rampant* (standing up on their hind legs).

As well as the *escutcheon*, or painted shield, early coats of arms featured a *crest*, a decorative figure on top of the knight's helmet. Crests were three-dimensional, and were usually made of lightweight material such as *cuir bouilli* (pronounced queer bwee-yee), or 'boiled leather,' a type of hardened leather treated with wax. The heraldic shield consisted of two elements, the background, called the *field*, and the design painted on it, which was known as the *charge*. Early charges were simple: a cross or stripe or chevron, or an animal, plant, weapon or other familiar image.

Heraldry was so called because it was regulated by the *heralds*, important officials who worked for kings and great lords as messengers and criers. Heralds listed all the knights who were vassals of their lord, and painted their *coat of arms* on long parchment scrolls, some of which still survive. The heraldic design was called a *coat of arms* because it was often embroidered or appliqued on the cloth coat the knight wore over his armor. Heralds also made up *tournament scrolls* listing all the knights entered in the tournaments held by their lords.

The earliest coats of arms were individual: each one identified a single knight. But before very long, by the fourteenth century, coats of arms had become associated with families, and were passed on from father to son. While their father was still alive his sons indicated their relationship by *differencing* their coat of arms with a conventional design displayed on top of the family coat. Coats of arms descend in the direct male line in families, except where there is no male heir, and a daughter becomes an *heraldic heiress*.

Since women did not wear armor, there was no practical reason for them to identify themselves with a coat of arms. Nevertheless, daughters wanted to indicate their family, and so they displayed their fathers' coat of arms. In the Middle Ages, if a noble girl married, her father's coat of arms was joined to her husband's, and their children bore both coats. In time, this led to multiple *quarterings*, with parents, grandparents' and great-grandparents' coats of arms being displayed on a single shield.

Coats of arms were primarily used to identify the knight riding into battle or the tournament, where his heraldic insignia extended to every part of his equipment. Especially in the tournament, where the participants wanted to present as dashing a picture as possible, the knight and his horse were both covered with heraldic designs. The horse's cloth coat and feathery plumes showed his master's colors, with the coat striped, checked or diapered (covered with lozenges) in accordance with the design of his owner's shield. The knight himself carried his heraldic design on his shield, his coat of arms or *surcoat*, and the pennant on the end of his lance. His helmet was topped off with a crest, which might resemble his shield or add another element to his design. Even dogs might wear a coat of arms — the Higgins Armory Museum's mascot, *Helmutt*, a boarhound wearing armor in sixteenth-century style to protect him against wild boar, displays the shield and plumes of his master, the Emperor Maximilian I!

Coats of arms became badges identifying aristocratic families, and are still used today. The College of Arms in London regulates British coats of arms, and many other European countries have their own heraldic officers who decide disputed claims to coats of arms, and regulate the granting of new coats.

Heraldic Activities: Things to Remember in Heraldic Design

Color Rule In heraldry, colors are called *tinctures*. The colors used are red, blue, green, black, purple. Heraldic colors are deep-toned, not pastel, so they are easy to see at a distance.

White and yellow are also used, but they are not considered tinctures because they represent the metals silver and gold.

Heraldry observes a color rule: white and yellow must never touch, and white or yellow must separate every other color. In other words, two *metals* must never touch each other, and neither may two *tinctures*.

To understand this rule, we must remember the original purpose of coats-of-arms: they were to enable knights to identify armed men riding towards them across an open field. In sunlight, or in twilight, the glint of silver and gold resemble each other, while the other colors all look indistinguishably dark. By using the shine of metals to separate the colors, the design of the coat-of-arms stands out and can be identified at a distance.

An easy way to observe this rule is to choose white or yellow as the field color, and make all charges out of other colors.

Symbolism of Coat-of-arms Designs Students may choose charges that symbolize one or more of the following:

1. Admired qualities Medieval coats-of-arms use animals, weapons and other images to express qualities they claimed: the lion for strength, the eagle for power, the stag for speed, the wolf for fierceness. Castles represented security and strength, battle-axes, power and might.

2. Ethnic affiliation Many countries are associated with a particular image: United States the bald eagle, France the *fleur-de-lis* or lily, Ireland the shamrock or harp, England the lion, Germany, Poland and Russia, the twin-headed eagle. Japanese students may want to use traditional *mon* images of stars, flowers or diamonds — note the hood ornaments of Mitsubishi or Subaru cars! African-Americans may choose the colorful patterns of *kente* cloth.

3. Place in family — Marks of Cadency While their father was living, sons indicated their relation to him by *differencing* their shield with a *mark of cadency*. See the illustration for a list of traditional images to show your place in the family, as the first through sixth child. These marks are placed at the center top of the shield.

The eldest child is indicated by the *label*, which is a white badge shaped like a bridge with 3, 5 or 7 legs. The second child is indicated by a crescent sitting on its back; the third by a *mullet*, which looks like a star but represents a spur. The third child is shown by a *martlet*, a small bird, the fifth by a ring called an *annulet*, and the sixth by a *fleur-de-lis*, or lily.

HERALDIC CHARGES

HERALDIC SHIELDS AND CRESTS

PLACE IN FAMILY
MARKS OF CADENCY

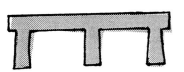

FIRST SON
A LABEL

SECOND
A CRESCENT

THIRD
A MULLET

FOURTH
A MARTLET

FIFTH
AN ANNULET

SIXTH
A FLEUR-DE-LIS

MARK IS PLACED 2 INCHES FROM THE TOP CENTER OF SHIELD

CANTING ARMS

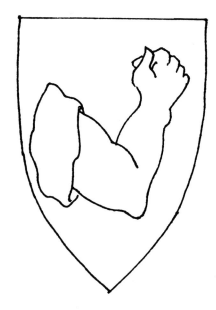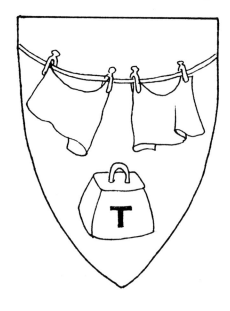

LOUIS ARMSTRONG   MARTHA WASHINGTON

4. Career interests Medical careers are indicated by the caduceus, twin serpents entwined around a staff, or by a serpent alone, the charge that traditionally represents wisdom. Teaching could be represented by a quill, or an apple. Engineering, carpentry and construction are symbolized by their particular tools, science by a flask, and so on.

5. Canting Arms *(See lefthand page)* Some of the earliest coats-of-arms are puns on the family name: the Bowes-Lyon family of Scotland has a coat made up of *bows* and *lions*, for instance, the Trumpingtons have *trumpets,* and the Oakleys have *oak-leaves.*

6. Motto A motto is a phrase to live by such as, *In God we Trust,* and *Live Free or Die.* Coats-of-arms include a motto, and students may choose to write one for themselves, which may be written on the shield or banner, or on a scroll of paper to be hung under or over the shield.

Activities

4-1. Design a Heraldic Pennant
Needs:
Construction paper in several colors.
Paper - pencil- ruler - scissors - glue.

Draw a pennant, 12 inches by 18, swallow-tailed or triangular (see illustration).
Choose your *charges* and draw them on construction paper.
Cut them out and glue them on the pennant.

Knights carried heraldic pennants on their lances.

4-2. Design and Make a Heraldic Banner
Needs:
Felt or other unpatterned fabric, approximately 17 by 22 inches
Different colored scraps of felt or other fabric
2-foot dowel
2-foot cord
Fabric glue
Needle and thread
Paper - pencil - scissors - ruler - straight pins
Draw the shield shape on your fabric and cut it out. This is your *field.*
Use pins to mark off a line four inches below the top of your shield. All of your design must fall below this line.
Design your coat-of-arms on paper (note the color rules and suggestions above). Cut out each *charge* from fabric scraps and sew or glue them on the field.

Fold the top of the shield down two inches at the back. Stitch along the line you have marked.

Insert the dowel. Tie the cord to its ends.

Make a Heraldic Shield ➡

4-3. How to Make a Heraldic Shield

Needs:

Corrugated cardboard, approximately 15 by 22 inches
Construction paper, same size as shield
Different colored scraps of construction paper
1 foot of sewing elastic
4 brass brads
Optional: "silver" or "gold" sticky tape
Masking tape
Glue - scissors - pencil - paper - ruler

Draw the shield shape on your cardboard and cut it out.

Cut the elastic into a 5 inch and 7 inch piece. These are your grips: the smaller one is for your wrist, and the larger one for your forearm. Attach them to the shield with brass brads. Flatten the ends of the brads well and cover them with masking tape.

Put your shield on the construction paper, draw its outline, and cut it out.
Glue it to the side of the shield with the masking tape. This is your *field*.

Design your coat-of-arms on paper (note the color rules and suggestions above). Cut out each charge from paper scraps or "silver" or "gold" foil and glue them on the field.

Vocabulary Words for Chapter Five

barrel helm	field
canting arms	great helm
charge	heraldry
coats of arms	lions rampant
crest	mark of cadency
cuir bouilli	motto
differencing	parchment
dynasty	quartering
escutcheon	tinctures

Chapter Five Word Search ➡

HERALDIC PENNANTS

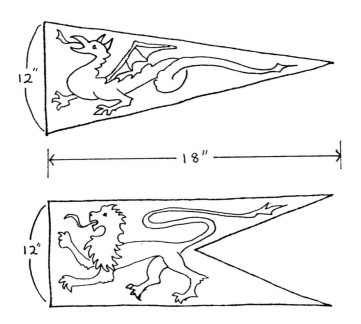

12"

18"

12"

TOURNAMENT TREE

Picture the Middle Ages page 40a

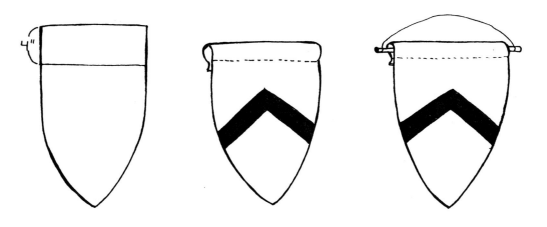

HOW TO MAKE A BANNER

HOW TO MAKE A SHIELD

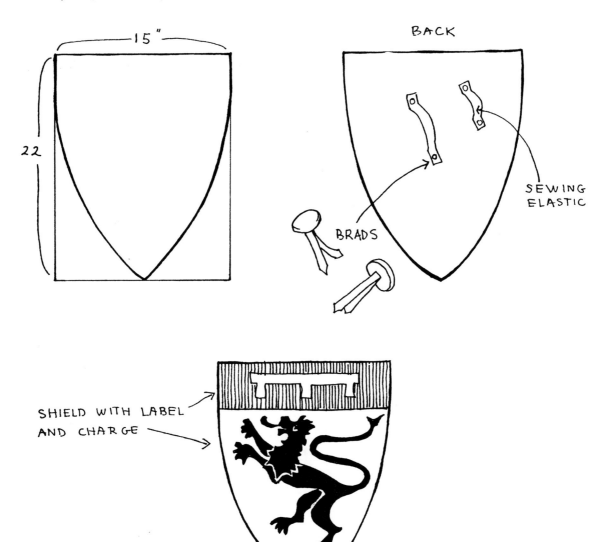

15"

22

BACK

SEWING
ELASTIC

BRADS

SHIELD WITH LABEL
AND CHARGE

The World of Heraldry Word Search

The words run forwards, backwards, up and down!

```
E   S   C   U   T   C   H   E   O   N

C   R   O   L   O   C   E   Q   U   X

N   L   A   T   E   M   R   U   S   C

E   O   T   T   O   M   A   A   Y   R

R   E   O   N   O   I   L   R   C   E

E   G   F   I   E   L   D   T   N   S

F   R   A   R   U   F   R   E   E   T

F   A   R   O   S   E   Y   R   D   A

I   H   M   G   N   I   T   N   A   C

D   C   S   E   L   G   A   E   C   D
```

Word List

Word	Clue
Cadency	.... badge to indicate bearer's place in family
Canting (Arms)	.... arms that pun visually on family name
Cat	.... popular charge
Charge	.... design on coat of arms
Coat of Arm	.... design identifying individual or family
Color	.... important component of coat of arms
Crest	.... identifying badge worn on top of helmet
Difference	.... small change made to coat of arms
Eagle	.... popular charge
Escutcheon	.... shield
Field	.... background of coat of arms
Fur	.... component of many coats of arms
Heraldry	.... hereditary system of identifying individuals and families by visual badges, controlled by heralds
Lion	.... popular charge
Metal	.... component of many coats of arms
Motto	.... brief inspiring phrase, often used on coats of arms
Quarter	.... division of coat of arms, representing one branch of family
Rose	.... popular charge

monastic life

Chapter Six

The Monastery: Monks & Nuns, Schools & Scholars

People and Possessions — Monastic Life *(Display and discuss illustration on lefthand page)*
In the upper left picture, two monks sit with books. One is a scribe, holding a quill pen, and a scraper with which to erase any mistakes he might make. The other monk is reading aloud, with his finger pointing to a word.

The upper right picture shows an *abbot*, the monk in charge of the abbey. (A nun in charge of an abbey is an *abbess.*) The abbot's rank is shown by his robe, resembling a bishop's: he carries a *crozier*, a ceremonial shepherd's crook, as an indication he should care for his flock as a shepherd cares for his sheep. He is speaking to a young monk.

In the lower left, a monk is teaching a class of boys. He is seated in a big chair, and holds a rod of birch twigs, the teacher's insignia. Boys sit on the floor, reading from books. One of them is reading to the teacher.

In the lower right, nuns and a young girl postulant are shown in their choir stalls in church, singing the psalms or reading their breviaries. They belong to a well-to-do order, so each nun has her own book. Because they spent so many hours each day in choir, their stalls have *misericords*, small projecting ledges on which they may lean instead of having to stand.

Monastic Life In the early Middle Ages, when nomadic tribes were fighting over the remains of the old Roman Empire, few parts of Europe were as peaceful as the remote lands where the Roman legions had never been. Such a place was Ireland, which was converted to Christianity in the fifth century by St. Patrick (circa 385-461), who had been brought there from the continent in boyhood as a slave. After escaping and becoming first a priest and then a bishop, Patrick voluntarily returned to bring the new religion to his former captors, who were pagans.

The High King of Ireland accepted Christianity at Tara, and the other kings soon followed suit. As his religion spread, Patrick encountered an organizational problem. In continental Europe the Christian church was organized around cathedral towns, ruled by bishops. But Ireland was a rural society, without towns, and needed a different kind of administration. Monasteries, religious communities of men (monks) or women (nuns), which were usually placed in the most remote possible locations, were ideal centers of administration for a rural land.

Monasteries had existed in the Christian church from early times, and they were soon established in Ireland. Most early medieval monasteries were Benedictine, that is, they followed the rule of St. Benedict of Nursia, an Italian monk who died about 543. The Benedictine rule called for a life dedicated to God through prayer and work. Each monastery was self-supporting, living off the food grown on its lands, and making all the goods the monks needed in their own workshops. Major monasteries were ruled by an abbot, and were called abbeys; smaller monasteries known as priories were created as offshoots of abbeys, and were ruled by priors.

The monastic life was frugal: food was strictly rationed, luxuries were shunned, and each hour of the day was filled with an allotted task. Monks and nuns took three major vows, of poverty, chastity and obedience. Poverty meant that no individual monk or nun could possess any property or goods; chastity bound them to leading a celibate life; and obedience required them to follow the monastic rule and their superior's orders.

Even though individual monks owned nothing, the order collectively could possess property and goods. Gifts and bequests from well-to-do aristocrats and merchants made monasteries wealthy. Through thriftiness and sound farming practices their lands became ever more valuable. By the late Middle Ages, monasteries controlled tens of thousands of acres of land throughout Europe, and their churches possessed gold and silver vessels and art work of all kinds.

The Monastic Day Monks pray many times each day and night, at special times known as *hours*. Starting in the early morning and ending during the night, the services held at these *hours* are called Matins, Lauds, Prime, Terce, Sext, Nones, Vespers and Compline. Because they needed to arise in the night to go to church to say the prayers of Compline, the dormitory where monks slept was usually built next to their church, often over the chapter house where the whole community met regularly to read a chapter of their monastic rule, and to discuss matters of communal concern.

Books of Hours In the late Middle Ages lay people took to saying some of the prayers chanted by monks at these hours, and prayer books containing excerpts from the monastic prayers became popular among lords and ladies. These *Books of Hours* were often beautifully illustrated. Among the most famous is the *Tres Riches Heures* (pronounced Tray Reesh Er — "Very Rich Hours") painted by the Limbourg Brothers circa 1415 for the Duke of Berry, France.

Monasteries were Farms, Inns and Hospitals Monasteries were required to be self-sufficient: they had to produce the food and other goods needed by their members, and care for all their needs. Frequently established on marshy or poor lands donated by landowners, monasteries pastured sheep, whose wool they needed. Their frugal and hard-working farming methods tended to improve whatever land they were granted, so that by the late Middle Ages monastic lands covered a large area of desirable arable land.

Just as they did not set out to become profitable farmers, but ended up farming thousands of acres, so monks did not intend to enter the hotel business, but in an age without safe shelter along the roads, felt obliged to offer hospitality to pilgrims and honest travelers who passed their way. Thus monasteries became established on major pilgrim routes, for example, from Paris and northern Europe to the great shrine of Saint James (Sant'Iago) at Compostela, in northern Spain.

The first hospitals in Europe were established in monasteries, where monks and nuns knowledgeable in herbal cures tended not only to their own sick, but also to the sick of the neighborhood. So monasteries, which had been established to allow their members to withdraw from the world to serve God, ended up serving mankind as well.

Monastic Scriptoria Monks and nuns were required to read an extensive compilation of prayer and scripture each day, from a book called a *Breviary* (pronounced breev-iary). This meant that monks and nuns had to know how to read, and it also meant that each monastery needed to have a large number of bibles, breviaries and other service books available. Writing therefore became an important skill necessary for every monastery, and since what was being copied was the Word of God, it was considered suitable to write it as beautifully as possible. The room in the monastery dedicated to copying books was called the *scriptorium*, plural *scriptoria*, which means writing room.

TYPICAL MONASTERY PLAN

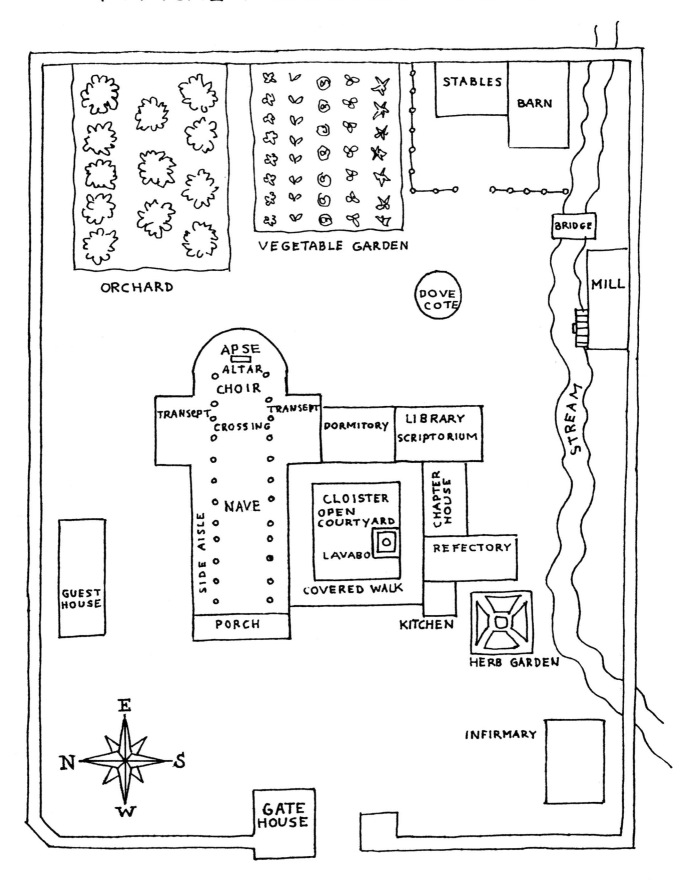

ORCHARD

VEGETABLE GARDEN

STABLES

BARN

BRIDGE

MILL

DOVE COTE

STREAM

APSE
ALTAR
CHOIR
TRANSEPT
TRANSEPT
CROSSING

DORMITORY

LIBRARY
SCRIPTORIUM

NAVE

SIDE AISLE

CLOISTER
OPEN
COURTYARD

LAVABO

CHAPTER HOUSE

REFECTORY

COVERED WALK

PORCH

GUEST HOUSE

KITCHEN

HERB GARDEN

INFIRMARY

E
N
S
W

GATE HOUSE

monastic life

Medieval Manuscripts Medieval books are called *manuscripts*, which means 'written by hand,' and the writers who copied them are called *scribes*. Once a manuscript was written, artists called *illuminators* labored to decorate it with beautiful patterns, scrolls, interlaced initials, and complete pages of color and line, designed to evoke the beauty of heaven.

So the copying of books became a major form of the work that St. Benedict's rule demanded, and monasteries became crucial centers of learning which preserved not only church service books, but also books written by the ancient Greeks and Romans. Ancient science, philosophy and literature were preserved, therefore, in remote sites by religious men and women whose prime concern was not with learning but with observing the rule of their Benedictine order. (Other ancient texts were preserved half a world away, in libraries of learned Arabs.)

From Ireland, home of some of the earliest monasteries in western Europe, monks traveled to Scotland, and founded monasteries there; and from Scotland, other monks spread to England and east to the continent. Irish monks, and Irish manuscripts, are found in the seventh century as far away from home as St. Gall in Switzerland, and monks from the monasteries founded by the Irish in Scotland and England were teaching at Emperor Charlemagne's court in the eighth century.

Monastic Schools and Scholars Monasteries developed schools to train their young monks and nuns in reading and writing, singing and music, and Latin and Greek, the languages in which church books were written. In western Europe, Latin was the language of all official business. When an illiterate king, such as Charlemagne, needed to send a letter or draft a document, he had a church-man act as his secretary. So the monastic schools found themselves training clerks for the royal courts, as well as priests for the church.

Perceptive kings and lords appreciated the value of literacy, and Charlemagne himself tried to learn to read as an old man, keeping a book near his pillow to practice on when he could not sleep. Lords like Charlemagne had their sons taught by learned monks; some royal children were even sent away to monasteries to be taught, and royal younger sons or daughters might spend their whole lives there. But you did not have to be royal to go to school in the monastery. Monasteries accepted applicants from among all free men and women, boys and girls. The monastic life was one of the few ways in which a medieval youth from a poor family could rise in the world. Educated in the monastic school, a clever young man could become an important administrator either within the monastic family or in the secular world of its feudal overlord.

Oblates Children were given to monasteries by their parents or guardians, as *oblates*, from a Latin word meaning *gift*. Some oblates were dedicated to God's service because of a vow taken by their parents, for example in thanks to God for a cure from disease. When they became adults, oblates had a choice between leaving the monastery or taking the permanent vows that bound them to its rule forever.

Children's lives and careers were always regulated by their parents in the Middle Ages; if not given to a monastery, they might be bound as apprentices to a particular trade. Parents who could not feed or educate their children themselves sometimes sold them into indentured servitude for a number of years. Even among aristocrats, the lives of sons were customarily decided for them: the oldest son was the heir, and inherited his father's lands and rank; often the next son had a choice of a military career or a career in the church, with the third son getting which ever of these careers his older brother had rejected; while the fourth son was apprenticed to some trade.

Suger One of the best-known oblates was the French monk Suger (1081-1151, pronounced Soo-zhair). Suger's parents were peasants belonging to the royal abbey of Saint-Denyis (pronounced San-Den-ee), outside Paris. They gave their son to the abbey as a young boy, and he was educated in the monastic school, where his classmates included the sons of the French royal family. Clever and hard-working, Suger did well in school, and chose to remain in the monastery as an adult. Elected abbot, he reformed the house and re-built the abbey church, creating the first known structure in the Gothic style of architecture. When King Louis VII left for the Second Crusade in 1147, he appointed Suger as head of his council of regents. So, through giving him away to the monastery, his poor illiterate parents had made it possible for Suger to become the ruler of his country!

Monastic Scholars As the Middle Ages advanced and learning increased, monks were among the foremost scholars in the new universities. The most famous medieval philosopher was St. Thomas Aquinas (1225-74), an Italian Dominican *friar*. Friars were members of the Franciscan or Dominican orders, founded in the late thirteenth century by St. Francis, patron of animals, and St. Dominic. Friars differed from other monks because they regarded preaching to the general populace as their prime responsibility, and frequented parish churches and market squares, rather than withdrawing to a life of personal prayer in monastic seclusion. St. Thomas studied Aristotle, and applied his principles of reasoning to religious knowledge; the *Summa Theologica* is his monumental work of theology and philosophy, still interesting and valuable today.

Other important medieval scholars included the scientists St. Albertus Magnus (1193?-1280), a German Dominican friar who taught St. Thomas Aquinas, and whose writings include studies of botany and metallurgy; and the English Franciscan friar Roger Bacon (1214?-1294?), who studied alchemy, and was ahead of his age in regarding precise observation and experiment as the roads to knowledge. Roger Bacon has been credited with inventing gunpowder.

New Monastic Orders Apart from the friars, other new monastic orders sprang up in the later Middle Ages. Their founders were often inspired with a desire for a stricter life than the existing abbeys offered. Among these reformed orders were the Cluniacs, founded in 910 at Cluny in France. Independent of local bishops, the Cluniacs stressed learning and music, and formed a highly disciplined order which attracted thousands of members, and large donations in land and goods.

Another reform movement led to the founding of the Cistercians in 1098, also in France. Known as the White Monks from their unbleached wool habit (a *habit* is a religious uniform), Cistercians were famous sheep farmers, and built churches all over Europe that are all recognizably the same, in a severe elegant early Gothic style. Their most famous member is St. Bernard of Clairvaux (1090?-1153), who preached the Second Crusade and argued with Abbot Suger against the propriety of lively pictorial sculpture in monasteries.

In comparing his contemporaries to the ancient Greeks and Romans, St. Bernard said: *we are as pygmies on the shoulders of giants*; meaning that although medieval people had less learning than the ancients, and needed to support themselves on ancient wisdom, still because of their Christian faith they could see farther than the wise men of old.

Saints and Relics In the Middle Ages, people believed that saints, deceased people who were honored for the holiness of their lives, could help the living by interceding for them with God. Even miraculous cures and other impossible events could be achieved if a saint were so disposed. How did one convince a saint to intercede on one's behalf? One way was to honor the saint by visiting his or her tomb, or the place where their *relics* were. *Relics* were bodily remains of the saint, or things they had touched, or that had been touched by their remains.

Frequently, a saint's body was divided up between many different shrines, so pilgrims had a choice of places to visit. The most revered relics were those connected with Christ himself. St. Louis (King Louis IX of France), brought back a relic of the True Cross, on which Christ was crucified, to Paris, and built the exquisite *Sainte Chapelle* (Holy Chapel — pronounced sant-sha-pel) to hold it in suitable splendor.

The possession of an important relic ensured large attendance at a shrine, and large donations, so monasteries and churches vied anxiously to get the best possible relics, occasionally even stealing them! Reliquaries are among the most beautiful of medieval art objects, boxes of precious metals and stones to hold the piece of bone, or sometimes statues in the shape of the relic — an arm, for example, or a head.

Activities

6-1. Illuminate your initial. Use the illustrations here as an example.

6-2. Make a manuscript. Take two sheets of plain white or tan paper, and fold them in half to make four pages. Write a story about a medieval person on these pages, adding more paper if you need. Cut out a cover for your book from a brown paper bag, and paint and letter the title on it. Sew your book together.

6-3. Write a letter that Suger might have sent to his parents, soon after he went to live in the abbey. How will he describe his new life? Will the food be better? The church beautiful? The rules strict? (Their parish priest will read the letter aloud to his parents.)

6-4. Look at the picture, *Monastic Life*. It shows monks and nuns praying, working, and preaching. Now look at the monastery plan. What was a day like in the monastery? Write a story about one particular day. Is it a feast day, with long church services, and a special dinner? Or is it a fast day, with very little food? What time of year is it? What is happening on the farm? The Benedictine rule required monks to work and pray; which kind of work is yours?

Topics for Discussion

6-5. Have a debate between Abbots Suger and Bernard of Clairvaux, on whether it is right to fill monasteries and churches with sculpture, painting and stained glass that will remind people of religious stories, as Suger believed, or whether churches and monasteries should be plain austere places for contemplation, as Bernard believed.

6-6. Was if fair for parents to give their children to monasteries? Remember that all medieval parents decided what work their children would do, and whom they would marry. By giving them away, the parents were losing a helper to work on their farm or craft. On the other hand, some aristocratic parents or guardians who gave their children to a monastery might be eager to banish an heir, so they could claim their fortune or land. Debate this question.

More Topics for Discussion & Vocabulary ➡

6-7. Joan of Arc claimed holy voices told her to leave her home and family, go to the castle where the prince was, and persuade him to give her charge of an army to lead against her country's enemies. If a teenage girl today left home, went to the Pentagon, insisted on speaking to the Chiefs of Staff and told them she had divine knowledge about how to solve the country's problems, how would they react? Have a debate between Joan's supporters and the Joint Chiefs of Staff and their followers.

Vocabulary Words for Chapter Six

abbess
abbot
book of hours
breviary
chapter house
Compline
crozier
habit
illuminator
Lauds
manuscript
Matins
misericord
monastic hours
monastic
Nones
oblate
Prime
quill
relics
scribe
scriptorium
Sext
Terce
Vespers

The Monastic World Word Search

The words run forwards, backwards, up and down!

```
M   O   N   K   E   A   N   T   H   F
O   X   U   R   T   R   C   O   O   A
N   E   N   T   A   U   L   B   U   T
A   B   E   L   L   L   O   B   R   C
S   C   R   I   B   E   I   A   E   I
T   H   K   O   O   B   S   Y   T   D
E   O   H   A   B   I   T   E   P   E
R   I   B   R   E   H   E   B   A   N
Y   R   A   I   V   E   R   B   H   E
P   R   I   O   R   Y   X   A   C   B
```

Word List

Abbey	....	house where monks or nuns lived, ruled by an abbot
Abbot	....	monk chosen to rule an abbey
Bell	....	rung to mark hours for prayer
Benedict	....	founder of major order of monks, Benedictines
Book	....	writing was a major monastic activity
Breviary	....	prayer book read each day by monks and nuns
Chapter	....	of the Rule, read aloud each day in Chapter House
Choir	....	group of monks who sang at church services
Cloister	....	open courtyard connecting monastery buildings
Habit	....	uniform worn by monks and nuns
Herb	....	monasteries had great herb gardens, used to treat the ill
Hour	....	monastic hours of prayer — nones (it became *noon*), terce, prime, vespers
Monastery	....	house lived in by monks or nuns
Monk	....	man dedicated to the service of God in a monastic order
Nun	....	woman dedicated to the service of God in a monastic order
Oblate	....	child given to a monastery by his parents
Prior	....	monk in charge of a priory
Priory	....	house where monks lived, subordinate to an abbey
Rule	....	written order of life for each monastic order
Scribe	....	person skilled in writing, often a monk or nun

On the manor

Chapter Seven

The Manor: Farming, Food & Feasting

People and Possessions — On the Manor *(Display and discuss illustration on lefthand page)*
The main picture shows a farm scene. The housewife milks a cow, while a shepherd holds a lamb. In the background a woman feeds chickens with grain, while another woman makes butter in a churn.

Beneath this picture, the illuminated initial shows a man sowing seed. Beneath him, another man plows with a horse and the late medieval high-wheel plow. Horses began to supplant oxen as draft animals in the twelfth century, because they could work much faster.

Along the bottom margin, a bee skep is surrounded by bees. Honey was the primary sweetening available in the Middle Ages, and *mead*, an alcoholic drink made from fermented honey was a popular beverage.

Along the left border, the sails of an up-to-date fourteenth century windmill revolve, while a farmer approaches it with his bag of grist (grain). In the top border, another farm hand picks grapes.

The Manor The manor was a legal entity, like a town, but consisted of farm lands and houses held by the *lord of the manor* as vassal of a greater lord. The manor's inhabitants, besides the lord and his family, consisted of *yeomen*, who were free to leave if they wanted, and *peasants*, who were divided into two classes, *free* and *unfree,* or *serfs*. All peasants belonged to the manor, although free peasants had a measure of personal independence. Like a castle, the manor was largely self-sufficient in the early Middle Ages. The lord of the manor ruled his people according to local manorial law and tradition, and the manor folk farmed its lands and carried out all the crafts necessary to its life.

Peasants' Revolts Peasants worked hard for the lord of the manor, and periodically their grievances resulted in uprisings which often led to an improvement in their condition. By the late Middle Ages, many peasants had become prosperous, living in solid stone houses like the one attributed to Joan of Arc's family in the village of Domremy in Loraine. Some poor knights were content to have their daughters marry prosperous peasants, which shows that the richer peasants mingled socially with the lower aristocracy.

A Banquet in the Castle ➡

People and Possessions — A Banquet in the Castle *(Display and discuss illustration on next page)* In the square picture, we see the *high table* at a banquet. The lord and lady preside, flanked by a taster or jester. Across from them sit two important visitors. A carver kneels to present a roast fowl, and an interested dog waits for its turn. Another server offers a bowl of fruit. On the table we see breads, pitchers of wine, a saltcellar (the covered box), a knife, a spoon and a goblet.

Beneath this picture, a young knight and lady entertain the guests with music. She plays the harp, and he plays the lute, as they sing. On the table behind them can be seen a small jewel chest, and an hourglass, an important way to tell time in the Middle Ages, together with the sundial and measured candles — mechanical clocks were not invented until the fourteenth century.

Nearby, a woman stitches at an embroidery hoop, while a cat plays with her thread. In the back of the hall, a falconer wearing a leather gauntlet takes his bird from its perch.

Food Production Food production in the Middle Ages was a constant problem, and even the rich and noble were helpless in the face of famine. Diet was simple, and almost totally bound by the seasons. Food was produced in one of four ways. It was either grown in local gardens, raised on local farms, or gathered or hunted in the forests. Mushrooms, nuts and berries gathered in the woods and hedgerows were an important part of the winter diet. Poaching, the illegal hunting of the lord's game in his forest, was strictly forbidden to the peasantry and strictly punished, often by death. The enforcement of laws against poaching was a constant source of misery since poor people inevitably stole to live.

The methods of preserving food for the winter were drying and salting. Salt was such an important staple, essential to survival, that its price was kept high and its production was often reserved by the king as a royal monopoly. Hard fruits such as apples and pears were stored for the lean months, as were cabbages and root vegetables like beetroot, carrots, turnips and parsnips. Beans and peas were dried, and became an important source of protein in the winter and early spring. Alcoholic drinks such as ale and wine made use of cereals and fruit that would otherwise have perished. Fruits were also dried, and raisins and prunes were popular flavorings for meat dishes.

Most farm animals were slaughtered at the onset of winter, when pastures dried up and food had to be saved for breeding beasts. Fish was an important part of the medieval diet. The church forbade the eating of meat on all Fridays and on many other *fast days*, but permitted the eating of fish. Fish were kept alive until needed in fishponds, which are found in monasteries and castles; sometimes they connect to a moat or flowing river. Lent, the penitential season that precedes Easter, when eating meat was severely restricted by church law, coincided with the time of greatest food shortage, so that fasting then turned a necessity into a blessing.

Fantasy Food Nevertheless, whenever possible, and certainly for major festivals such as Christmas and Easter, and for weddings and court ceremonies, the castle and manor kitchens really turned out a feast, with dish following dish in a great surfeit of abundance. Appearance was important, and fantasy was loved. Vegetable salads were made up in strange and wonderful shapes, including landscapes and heraldic designs.

Strange beasts were invented by the cooks, who would sow together the head of a peacock and the back of a pig, to make a fantastic beast called a *cockatrice*, that was brought to the table with all its feathers on. Trick pies were sometimes the high point of a grand dinner. Live blackbirds would fly out when the pie was cut open, or musicians would step out, blowing trumpets. Even monasteries would create food fantasies for high feast days, making images of fish and meat from fruits and vegetables to brighten their vegetarian diet. ❖ ❖ ❖   **Chapter Seven Activities** ➡

A Banquet in the castle

Activities

There is information on putting on your own medieval feast in Chapter 12.

7-1. Feasts and Holidays. Discuss the different foods and celebrations students from different cultures enjoy. How many different foods do we all eat? What days do we celebrate? Birthdays, name days, New Year's, religious holidays, weddings? Are there any special plates, dishes, customs that are used on special occasions? Write a story about your favorite celebration.

7-2. Look at the picture *On the Manor*. Name all the different farming activities you can find. How many different kinds of food will they produce? Write out a menu using only these foods. What other medieval foods are missing? What seasons are shown in each of the pictures here?

7-3. Look at the picture *A Banquet in the Castle*. Identify all the people and things in the picture. What are all the dishes on the table? What foods are they eating? What activities are happening in the Great Hall apart from dining?

7-4. Suppose for dinner today all you could have was food grown, foraged or hunted within a 20 mile radius of your home, and available at the present time of year. What could you have? Plan the best possible dinner using only these local materials, and 3 imported spices. Remember - you might have some vegetables, fruits or dried meat in your cellar; but you cannot use any frozen or foreign foods, except the spices.

7-5. Keep a diary of all the foods and beverages you consume in a week. Then list them all on the board, dividing them into 2 columns: those you could have had if you lived in the Middle Ages, and those you could not! How many of the foods you eat are local? Does the ratio change with the seasons?

Topic for Discussion

7-6. What changes in society have made the great changes in our diet from medieval times? Are there any places in the world today where food consumption is still on the medieval pattern, local and seasonally scarce? Where are people still liable to periodic famine? Debate whether we in the prosperous countries have responsibility for people in other countries who are hungry, and if so, how can we best help them. And: how about people here at home — are any of them hungry? And if so, what should be done about it?

Vocabulary Words for Chapter Seven

manor	jester
grist	poaching
vassal	cockatrice
serf	mead
peasant	fast days
yeoman	

BAYEUX TAPESTRY

DETAIL OF EMBROIDERED DESIGN

Chapter Eight

Making Costumes and Armor

Early Medieval Dress: A.D. 300-1100

Men Men wore round-necked knee-length linen or woolen gowns belted at the waist, and sometimes covered by knee-length woolen cloaks. Their legs were covered by linen or woolen hose that were baggy, not knit or woven of stretchy material. Because they were baggy, the hose were cross-gartered, that is, bound by thongs in a criss-cross pattern. They wore short, soft leather boots. Their hair was uncovered, and tied with a band above the forehead, or a crown.

Women Women wore round-necked ankle-length linen or woolen gowns, belted at the waist, and sometimes covered by ankle-length woolen cloaks. Their hair was worn long, either free, held at the forehead by a band or crown, or bound up with ribbons in one or two criss-crossed braids. They could also wear a linen veil, hanging straight down the back.

Ornament Both men and women wore *torcs*, heavy bracelets and necklets of rigid gold, silver or bronze. Crowns were made of all these metals, and decorated with large colorful jewels. The edges of their cloaks or gowns could be trimmed with contrasting colored braid trimmed with large jewels. Women's belts were often tied at the waist, falling to their knees in a colorful single band.

Monks and Nuns Wore a long woolen or linen robe and gown, undecorated, in plain sober colors, black, white, gray or brown. They might wear a cross-shaped *scapular* of contrasting plain cloth hanging over their shoulders, and they might carry a wooden or metal cross. Nuns wore white or black linen veils to cover their hair. Monks wore their hair in the *tonsure*, a shaved circle around the crown of the head.

Warriors Early medieval warriors dressed like other men with the occasional addition of a simple leather breastplate to protect the torso. They carried a round or kite-shaped shield, a spear and a sword, and wore a conical helmet with a *nasal*, a protecting metal strip over the nose.

Late Medieval Dress: A.D. 1100-1400

Men Gowns lengthened below the knee; noblemen, churchmen and professional men like lawyers and physicians wore ankle-length gowns in the late Middle Ages. In the fourteenth and fifteenth centuries, young men wore short gowns to their hips over tight colorful hose - often with each leg a different color. The gown was belted at the waist. Men's hats were high-crowned and trimmed with fur or feathers. Merchants and craftsmen wore woolen hoods with long tails wrapped around their necks, called *liripipes*.

Women Dress became more elaborate after the thirteenth century. Ladies now wore sleeveless low-necked *kirtles* over their gowns, with cut-out sides revealing their slender waists. Jewelry became smaller and more delicate. Hats were worn by all married women. Unmarried girls wore their hair loose or flowing free from under a small often jeweled cap; ears were always covered. Ladies wore tall conical hats called *hennins*, or butterfly-shaped headdresses floating high over their heads. Veils often fell from these hats.

Making Medieval-style Costumes

Materials

Wool Most medieval clothing was made at home. Wool was the commonest material, since sheep were found all over the medieval world. Cloth making was an endless labor for women: an unmarried woman became known as a *spinster* from the spinning that filled her day. Women also wove cloth and made up the clothes. In towns, the cloth makers or *mercers* formed one of the most powerful guilds.

Linen The flax plant grows from as far south as Egypt all across Europe to Ireland and Belgium. Linen, the fine cloth that can be made from it, was and is prized for its comfortable smoothness and coolness. Medieval women made lightweight clothing from linen.

Cotton Grown in Africa, Asia and parts of extreme southern Europe, cotton was not available to most people in medieval Europe.

Silk Brought back from China by Marco Polo, silk was a highly-prized luxury fabric worn at court. The first pair of silk stockings brought to England is bright yellow, and was given to Queen Elizabeth I in the sixteenth century. Medieval merchants brought silk from the southeast to their northern customers.

Leather Used for shoes, boots, armor and heavy work clothes. Farmers and craftsmen wore leather aprons. Men-at-arms often wore leather armor such as the *jack*, a leather coat reinforced with iron plates.

Fur In cold drafty houses and castles, fur was worn by all who could afford it in winter. Rich men and women trimmed their gowns and robes with fur, and kings and queens wore robes of *ermine*, the winter coat of the stoat, white with gray markings, as a sign of rank.

Feathers Peacock and osprey feathers were used to decorate hats and helmets.

Color Most medieval clothing was made at home from wool or linen woven by the housewife and either undyed or dyed with vegetables. Undyed cloth was soft off-white, or if made of wool from a black or brown sheep, it might be gray, brown, or a dull black. Vegetable dyes give soft muted colors: onions make a soft orange, parsley makes a gentle green. Lichens make yellow and orange dyes, and so on. Poor people's clothing could come only from this narrow range of colors.

But we know from their brilliant stained glass windows and the glowing pages of illuminated manuscripts that medieval people loved bright colors, and at the court, where money was plentiful, kings and queens and their entourages revelled in brilliant clothing of scarlet, purple, and gold. Purple was the royal color because it was so rare; both it and scarlet were imported dyes made from small shellfish found in the Mediterranean.

Embroidery Royal and noble ladies were no less busy about making clothes than humbler women, but their time was spent not in the basics of spinning and weaving, but in the embroidering of magnificent pictures on clothing, church and court regalia, and household textiles. Embroidery was an important art form in the Middle Ages, with some of the most impressive being the *opus anglicanum*, or *English work*, which uses gold and silver thread to create raised designs of unsurpassed richness.

Bayeux Tapestry Despite its misleading name, the *Bayeux* (pronounced Bye-yuh) *Tapestry* is actually an example of medieval embroidery. A strip of linen two hundred and thirty feet long by about two feet wide, it shows the whole story of the invasion and capture of England by Duke William the Conqueror and his Norman knights in 1066 in a long continuous cartoon-like illustration. It has traditionally been attributed to Duke William's wife, Queen Matilda, and her ladies. Besides depicting the conquest, the Bayeux Tapestry gives an invaluably detailed pictorial account of eleventh-century life. *(See illustration on p. 54)*

Clothing the Medieval Person Could Not Wear

Lace Not made before the Renaissance. The earliest examples date from the end of the fifteenth century. Medieval women are sometimes shown wearing sheer veils or blouses that appear to be of lace; they are actually made of extremely fine linen or silk.

Knitting Unknown before the fifteenth century at the end of the period.

Stretch fabrics Medieval weaving could not make fabrics that stretched, so even hose should be shapeless and somewhat baggy.

Man-made fibers Nylon, polyester, dacron etc. are twentieth century conveniences!

Chemically-dyed fabric Lurid colors in strange shades do not look medieval!

Who Wears What: Easy Costumes for Play or Festival

Bishops Bishops wear a purple robe decorated with braid. A large jeweled cross hangs around the neck. They hold a crozier, a ceremonial version of a shepherd's crook, which can be made from a broom handle with a papier-mache crook at the top. Their hat is a mitre, a stiff hat made from two shield-shaped pieces of cardboard 12 inches high and 8 inches wide, stapled together at the sides, and decorated with paint or braid.

Children Children wear the same clothing as an adult in their station in life.

Craftsmen & Craftswomen They wear tunics in dull colors. The men's come to the knee, the women's to the ankle. Both wear aprons, and women wear veils. They carry tools of their trade.

Jesters Jesters wear a short tunic in bright colors, a soft cloth hat (see Hennin) with bells, and carry a Jester Stick - a 12 inch dowel with bells and crepe paper streamers stapled to one end.

Kings Kings wear a Robe in red or purple, richly trimmed with jewels and fur, and a golden Crown. They carry an *orb*, a round 6-inch ball topped with a cross and covered in aluminum foil, and *scepter*, a ceremonial mace, made by fixing a round aluminum-covered ball at the end of a 1-foot dowel.

Knights Knights wear a tunic called a surcoat, cross-gartered hose and helmet, and carry a shield and sword. The surcoat is a cloth knee-length tunic that covers the armor and protects it from rain and sun. The surcoat bears the knight's heraldic coat-of-arms on the chest and upper back.

Merchants They wear a tunic or robe in rich dark colors trimmed with fake fur. Their hats are made from second-hand men's or women's felt hats, decorated with feathers and braid. They carry their money in a soft leather purse slung over their shoulders.

Merlin Merlin wears a black robe trimmed with silver cloth or yellow felt cut-outs of the sun, moon and stars, with fake fur around the neck and down the front. He wears a black hennin decorated with zodiacal signs or stars, and carries a magic wand made from an 18 inch dowel ending in a star made of cardboard covered in aluminum foil.

Monks & Nuns They wear a robe in white, brown, gray or black, tied around the waist with a thick cord. They may carry or wear a large cross. Nuns wear a plain white or black veil.

Peasants Men wear a short tunic and cross-gartered hose in dull brown. Women wear a mid-calf length tunic in some faded soft color, not red or purple, with a white or off-white apron. Short veils are optional. Tears and tatters are *de rigeur*! They may carry a gardening spade or fork, or basket of vegetables or fruit, or a stuffed lamb.

Queens & Ladies Medieval ladies wear a gown in rich fabric in bright colors, with a decorated tall hat, the hennin. Queens wore gowns in red or purple, trimmed with jewels, fur and braid, with a golden crown instead of a hat.

Robin Hood He wears a belted green tunic. His green felt hat is made from two triangles of green felt, 18 inches wide by 10 inches high, stitched together and turned up in front. It is decorated with a feather. He carries a bow, and wears a quiver full of arrows on a rope slung around his shoulder. (His quiver can be made from two round oatmeal boxes taped together.) His men dress similarly. **Maid Marian** dresses in green also, like a peasant woman with flair — some woodsy braid or other decoration would be appropriate. She carries a bow and wears a quiver.

Students Students dress like clerics, in a plain dark robe ending below the knee. They may have cheery cross-gartered hose showing under the robe, however.

Costume patterns ➡

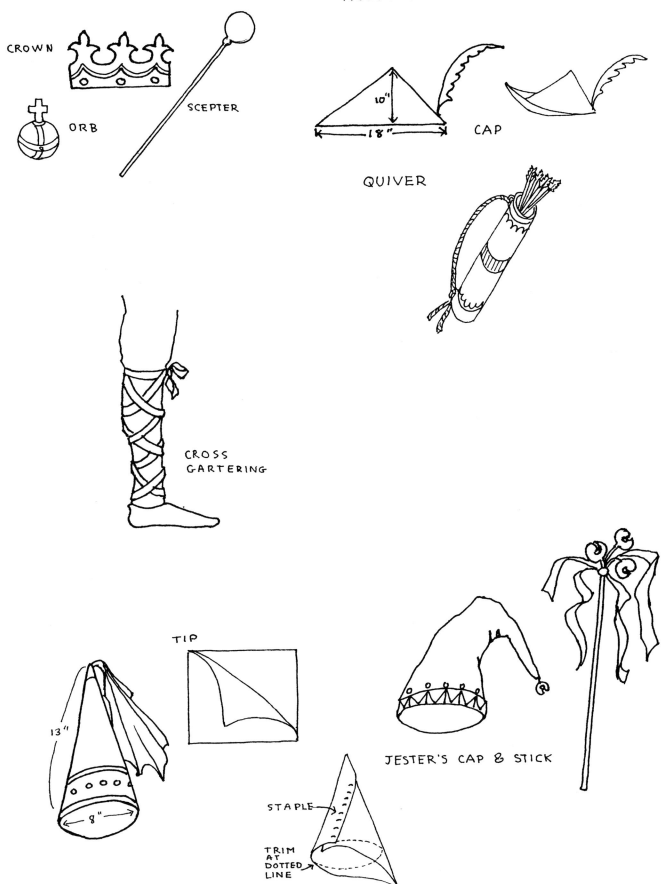

KING

CROWN

ORB

SCEPTER

ROBIN HOOD

10"

18"

CAP

QUIVER

CROSS GARTERING

TIP

13"

8"

JESTER'S CAP & STICK

STAPLE

TRIM AT DOTTED LINE

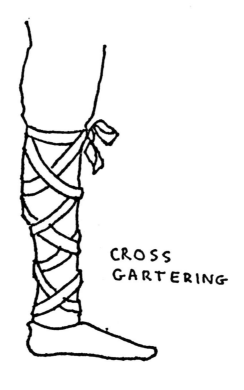

CROSS
GARTERING

CROWN

Medieval Costume Patterns

Cross-gartering

Needs:
- ✓ 2-3 yards of tape or ribbon, half or three-quarter inches wide.
- ✓ Plain long pants or plain kneesocks.

Steps:
1. The pants may be cross-gartered, or plain kneesocks may be worn over the pants and cross-gartered.
2. Shoes may be omitted. If needed, they should be plain dark leather. The "dorm-boot" style of slipper looks appropriate.
3. Since hose was baggy, it was tied to the leg with a strip of cloth starting just below the knee and ending at the ankle. Use 2-3 yards of ribbon or tape in a color that contrasts with the hose or pants being gartered.
4. Tie one end of the tape around the leg just below the knee, then wind it in a circular pattern down to the ankle. Go around the ankle and then wind it back up the leg to the knee, ending with a bow.

Crown

Needs:
- ✓ Cardboard, 6 x 24 inches.
- ✓ "Gold" or "silver" foil or paint.
- ✓ Duct tape. Staples.
- ✓ Optional: Fake jewels and glue.

Kings and queens in the Middle Ages wore golden crowns that were often shaped in a leafy or flower pattern.

Steps:
1. Measure around the wearer's head, then cut out a piece of cardboard 6 inches high and as wide as your head size, plus 3 inches.
2. Mark off 3 inches at one end. Draw your crown design on the cardboard, leaving the marked 3 inches blank.
3. Cut out your crown, and cover it with gold or silver foil, or gold or silver paint.
4. Fasten the crown together with duct tape on the inside, or staples, overlapping the 3 inch section.
5. Glue on jewels.

Gown

Needs:
- ✓ Length of cloth, plain or brocaded, 54 inches wide by 8-10 feet long. Old tablecloths or upholstery remnants can be used, but they should not have a printed pattern. The cloth must be twice the length of the wearer's shoulder-to-ankle measurement.
- ✓ Trimming: braid, fake fur, fake jewels.
- ✓ Belt (optional): 4-6 feet silk cord.
- ✓ Fabric glue. Needle and thread.

The gown is full-length and high-necked with long full sleeves. It should be worn over a long-sleeved plain-colored blouse. Slippers or plain-colored socks may be worn on the feet.

Steps:
1. Fold the fabric lengthwise. At the fold, measure in 20 inches from each side (A). From point A, measure down 10 inches (B).
2. Along each outer edge, measure down from fold 15 inches (C).
3. From point C, mark a line to point B. At the lower edge, measure in 10 inches on each side (D).
4. Cut and sew along lines C - B and B - D.
5. Neck opening: Measure in from sleeve ends 24 inches (E).
6. From center point, measure down 4 inches (F). Join F to E with a curved line. Cut E - F - E.
7. Belt: The gown may either hang straight or be belted with a long loose silk cord, knotted at the waist with the ends hanging down in front.
8. Trimming: Decorate neck opening, sleeve ends and hem with fake fur, fake jewels, and rows of braid or ribbons, attached with fabric glue or stitched on.

Hennin

Tall cone-shaped hat with a veil worn by ladies and magicians in the late Middle Ages. The jester's hat is a soft version of the hennin, hanging down to the shoulders rather than standing up.

A simple version can be made from stiff paper or poster board; a more durable hat is made from felt or heavy fabric over poster board. Merlin's hat is a black hennin, decorated with stars, moon and sun cut out of silver or gold foil and glued on. A jester's hat is made like a hennin from felt or other soft fabric in a bright color, but without any stiff cardboard; bells are sown on the tip or around the forehead.

Needs:
- ✓ Sheet poster board 22 x 28 inches (not needed for jester's hat).
- ✓ Quarter-yard of chiffon or other sheer fabric (not needed for Merlin's or jester's hat).
- ✓ Half-yard of braid.
- ✓ Duct tape.
- ✓ For jester's hat: Bells.
- ✓ For Merlin's hat: Silver or gold foil stars, sun and moon or zodiacal designs.
- ✓ Optional: Half-yard felt or upholstery fabric to cover hat.
- ✓ Fabric glue. Fake jewels. 1 yard Ribbon to tie under the chin.

Steps:
1. Take the poster board at one corner and fold it into a cone shape along the shorter side. Staple it at each end, and as far up the middle as your stapler will reach. Cut it around the end to even it, and make it 13 inches tall. The opening for the head should be 8 inches across. Cover the joint with duct tape on the inside.

Making a hennin, steps 2-5 ➡

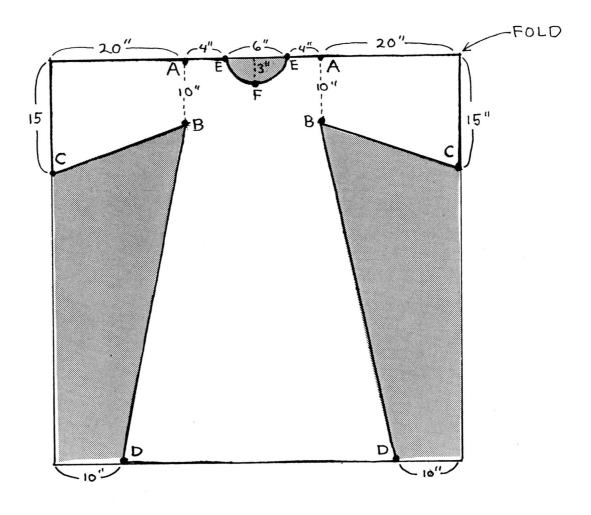

FOLD

20"   4"   6"   4"   20"

A   E   3"   E   A

10"   10"

15   15"

C   B   B   C

D   D

10"   10"

GOWN

ROBE

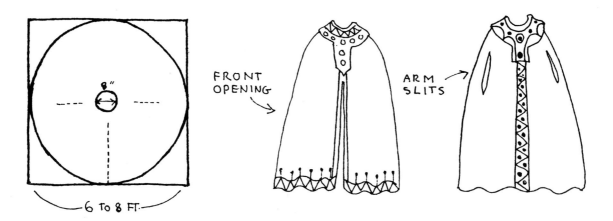

FRONT OPENING

ARM SLITS

6 TO 8 FT.

8"

TUNIC OR SURCOAT

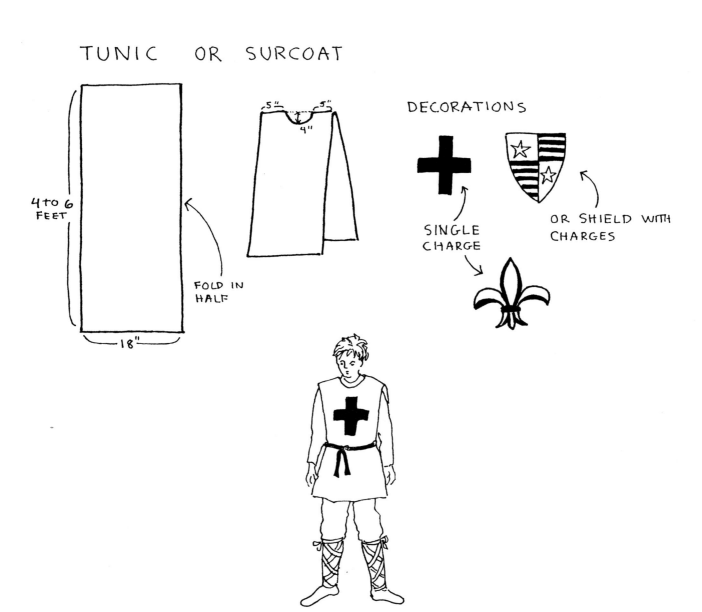

4 to 6 FEET

FOLD IN HALF

18"

5" 5"

4"

DECORATIONS

SINGLE CHARGE

OR SHIELD WITH CHARGES

2. Glue felt or other solid fabric over the hat, and trim to fit.
3. Gather the sheer fabric together at one end, and staple it to the top of the hat.
4. Glue braid around the end of the hat. Decorate with fake jewels.
5. If desired, punch a hole above each ear, and attach ribbon to tie under chin.

Robe

Needs:
✓ Fabric square, 6-8 feet across.
✓ Fake fur, braid, fake jewels.
✓ Needle and thread, fabric glue.

Steps:
1. A robe is made like a poncho, from a circle of fabric with a central opening for the head. Old tablecloths, bedspreads or sheets can be used, or burlap or fabric remnants can be stitched together to make a square.
2. Measure from the wearer's shoulders to ankles, then double the length. This is the size of the square piece of fabric needed.
3. Cut a circle from the square. Fold it in four to find the center; cut an 8 inch diameter circle for the neck opening.
4. Cut a 1-foot slit on each side, 12 inches down from the edge of the neck opening, for the arms. Or: slit the robe up the front, fastening it with a large colorful "jeweled" pin.
5. Decorate the robe with fake fur, braid, and fake jewels, sown or glued around the neck opening, hem, and down the front.

Tunic or Surcoat

Needs:
✓ Length of unpatterned cloth, 18 inches wide by 4-6 feet long. Burlap or inexpensive cotton remnants work well. The cloth must be twice the length of the wearer's shoulder-to-knee measurement. 36-inch-wide fabric may be cut in half the long way to make two surcoats from each length.
✓ Belt: 4-6 foot cord or tape to tie around waist.
✓ Coat-of-arms: Scraps of contrasting cloth or felt. Fabric glue (not school glue), or needle and thread.

Steps:
1. Fold fabric in half lengthwise.
2. Measure 5 inches in from each shoulder, and draw a curving line 4 inches down from the top edge at the fold. Cut along this line to make the neck opening.
3. The surcoat is decorated with a coat-of-arms on the chest and upper back.
4. The coat-of-arms may be a copy of the shield, made in felt or cloth, and glued or stitched on. A simple cross or stripe, 12 inches long, in a contrasting color is also effective. Remember - a stripe should run from the wearer's right shoulder to his left ribs. A stripe in the other direction is **a bend sinister,** and indicates illegitimacy. *(See Chapter Five for further suggestions)*
5. Under the tunic, men wear a plain long-sleeved knit shirt, and long plain pants that are cross-gartered. (Although they are anachronistic, knit shirts look best because they have plain collars and cuffs.)

How to Make a Knight's Breastplate

Needs:
- ✓ Corrugated cardboard 22 x 15 inches.
- ✓ 3 yards cord or heavy string.
- ✓ Scissors - pencil - crayons or paint - punch.

Steps:
1. Using the illustration as a pattern, draw the breastplate on your cardboard, and cut it out.
2. Look at pictures of armor, and design the decoration for your breastplate. You may want to copy your shield design.
3. Draw the design on the breastplate, and color it with crayons or paint. Armor is traditionally either left plain gray metal color, or painted black, or it may be stained with heat and acid to brown, blue or black. Chose one of these colors for the body of the armor, and then make your design in a contrasting color: silver, gold, red and black are all traditional.
4. With a blunt pencil or pencil end, press three grooves on the back of the breastplate lengthwise from neck to waist.
5. Fold gently along these grooves so the breastplate fits around your body. Punch 4 holes at the spots marked X.
6. Cut the cord in two equal lengths. Knot a cord through each shoulder hole, and thread it through the opposite waist hole.
7. Put the breastplate on with the cords criss-crossing on your back. Tie the ends in front.

How to Make a Knight's Helmet

Needs:
- ✓ 2 pieces of gray poster-board or railroad board.
- ✓ 28 x 11 inches and 16 x 6 inches.
- ✓ 2 yards crepe paper streamers in 2 or 3 colors.
- ✓ 5 brass brads.
- ✓ Half-yard duct tape.
- ✓ 8 inch circle of construction paper.
- ✓ Glue.
- ✓ Optional: "silver" or "gold" sticky tape.
- ✓ Scissors - pencil - crayons or paint - ruler - punch.

Steps:
1. Draw the helmet and visor patterns on the two pieces of poster-board, and cut them out. Draw the face opening on the helmet.
2. Cut thirteen 3-inch slits along one long side of the helmet.
3. Cut out the face opening in the helmet.
4. Punch three evenly-spaced holes along each short side of the helmet. The holes on one side should line up with the others so they may be fastened together.
5. Punch a hole at each end of the visor.
6. Cut three horizontal slits in the visor for visibility. Note: the wider side of the visor is the top.
7. Decorate the visor to match the helmet.

Making a Helmet, next steps, 8-16 ➡

HOW TO MAKE A KNIGHT'S BREASTPLATE

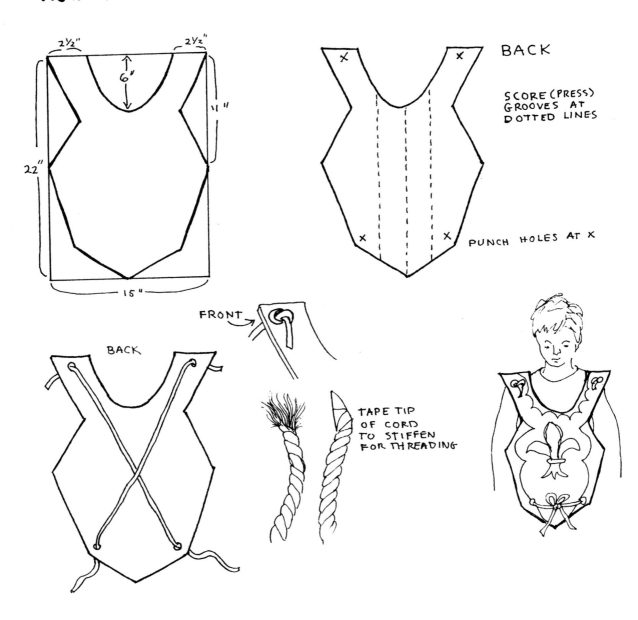

2½"   2½"

6"

1"

22"

15"

BACK

SCORE (PRESS) GROOVES AT DOTTED LINES

X   X

X   X

PUNCH HOLES AT X

FRONT

BACK

TAPE TIP OF CORD TO STIFFEN FOR THREADING

HOW TO MAKE A KNIGHT'S HELMET

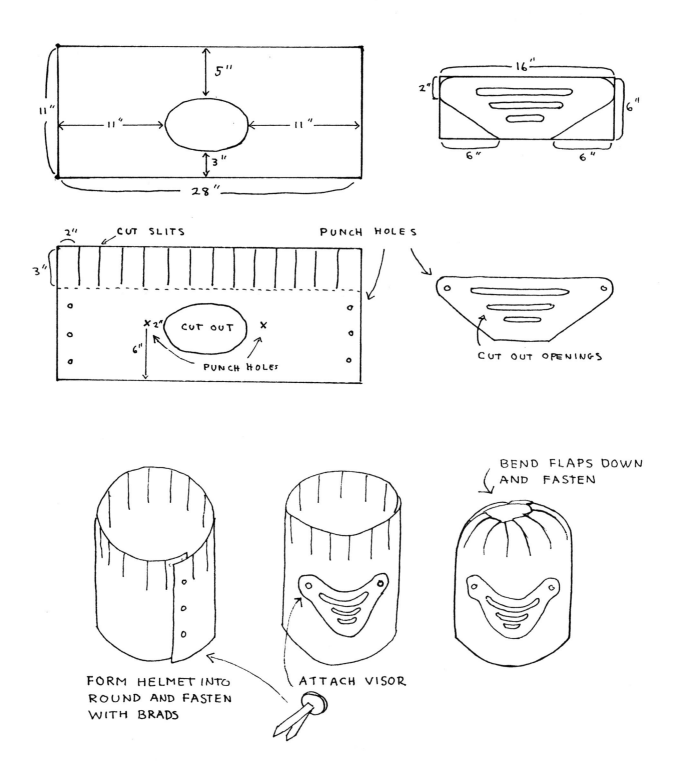

5"

11"   11"   11"

3"

28"

16"

2"   6"

6"   6"

CUT SLITS   PUNCH HOLES

2"

3"

X 2"   CUT OUT   X

6"   PUNCH HOLES

PUNCH HOLES

CUT OUT OPENINGS

BEND FLAPS DOWN AND FASTEN

FORM HELMET INTO ROUND AND FASTEN WITH BRADS

ATTACH VISOR

Picture the Middle Ages page 62b

8. Attach the visor to the helmet at the points marked X with a brass brad. Flatten the ends of the brads and cover with masking tape.

9. Design your helmet decoration to match or coordinate with your shield and breastplate. (Note: the slits indicate the top of the helmet)

10. Decorate your helmet with crayons or paint, or cut designs from foil tape.

11. Bend the helmet into a round by fastening the sides together.

12. Fasten the short sides of the helmet together with 3 brads fastened through the holes.

13. Flatten the ends of the brads and cover them and all the inside seam with duct tape.

14. Bend down the flaps in the top of the helmet and overlap them so they cover most of the top of the head.

15. Cut crepe paper streamers into 18 inch lengths. Hang them over face of helmet and tape the ends to center front of top.

16. Overlap adjoining flaps and hold helmet upside down on table. Cut two 8 inch lengths of duct tape and tape them inside helmet top to fasten flaps together. Cut an 8 inch circle from construction paper and glue it on outside top of helmet.

Flick crepe paper streamers back over helmet.

Vocabulary Words for Chapter Eight

cross-gartered

torc

tonsure

nasal

liripipes

hennin

kirtle

mercer

mitre

orb

surcoat

bend sinister

MINSTRELS   GALLERY

Picture the Middle Ages

Chapter Nine

Music and Dance in the Middle Ages

Music of the Church

Gregorian Chant Pope Gregory the Great (590-604) was known as a codifier and collector of the chants sung during the liturgy of the Mass. Eventually these chants, called *plainchants* or *plainsongs*, became known as *Gregorian chant* in his honor. The earliest church musicians had to balance form (plainchant) and function (the liturgical setting of the music).

Polyphony Plainchant played an important role as the root of religious polyphony during the Middle Ages. Out of the monophonic (one-voice) plainsong grew parallel organum, the earliest form of polyphony (many-voiced). This consisted of two voices moving in parallel motion. Eventually other voices were added to the voices singing in parallel motion. With the addition of other parts, polyphonic music began to exhibit more rhythmic and melodic independence.

The Mass In the Mass, the central service of the church, what had started as the chanting of the Psalm verses grew in the Middle Ages to a dialogue between two singers and eventually between two choirs. Most of the singing performed inside the church was performed without accompaniment. That is why we use the term *a cappella* for unaccompanied singing — it means "at the church". The only instruments allowed in the church were the organ, bells and harp.

Troping It was in the church that the practice of *troping* began, which was to add more and more music in the form of verses to the various sections of the Mass. To *trope* means to compose music to add to the Mass — it comes from the French word *trouver*, which means "to find". "Trouver" is also the root of such words as *troubadour* (England), *trouvere* (France), and *trovatore* (Italy). Troubadours and their foreign counterparts were people who made their living "finding" or composing music.

Religious Drama It was a small step to add acting to the sung dialogues in the Mass. A musical drama was born! In fact, these religious dramas are the root of today's operas. The congregation enjoyed watching these dramas during the Mass, and since most of them did not understand Latin, which was the language of the Mass, the dramas helped them to make sense out of what was going on.

In time, the church dramas grew to include stories from the Bible. But as time passed, the Church authorities decided these simple stories had became too loud, too colorful and too vernacular, and banned them from the Church.

The musical dramas were not stopped. They were simply moved to the square outside the church, where instruments were added to make them even more appealing.

Choir Books In the monastery, monks could be found painstakingly copying music into huge choirbooks, which had to be large enough for everyone in the choir to see, because it was too time-consuming to write out a book for each singer. Until 1473, when the first printed music became available, all music was copied by hand. Because the monks did the copying, much of the music of the Middle Ages which has survived to the present is sacred in origin.

Musical Notation It was during the Middle Ages that a system of notation was developed which allowed music to be written down. Unfortunately, it was never indicated in the manuscripts which part was to be played by a particular instrument or if the instruments were to double what the voices were singing. Scholars have concluded that instruments were indeed used for accompaniment. The only music which appears to have been written solely for instruments was dance music.

The music manuscripts of the Middle Ages looked very different from the music which we read today. The notes were shaped to indicate rhythm and sometimes there were more than five lines to a staff.

Music of the Town

Outside the church, music could be found in the villages and castles where it served as an accompaniment to dancing. Minstrels carried news about the countryside and provided information and entertainment. The ballad singer usually traveled alone, and bought and sold news and tales of heroic events.

The towns of the Middle Ages might be quiet, sleepy villages or bustling cities. Peddlers would be found in the marketplace, their street cries filling the air as they hawked their wares. Fairs brought many traveling entertainers into town. Jugglers, acrobats, dancers and instrumentalists added to the festive atmosphere. The coming and goings of pilgrims were a noisy occasion. Some pilgrims played bagpipes, hunting horns and harps, as recounted by Chaucer in his *Canterbury Tales*.

During the Christmas season it was the custom of poor folk to go round to the houses of the rich and sing. They would ask for a soul cake and drink. Upon receipt of these items, they in turn wished *wassail* or good cheer and good luck in the coming year to their benefactors.

Maypole In front of the church one might find a guild acting out an appropriate Bible story for the public. On the village green serfs, laborers and servants would meet to feast and dance. They would dance the same dances as those at court but in a more relaxed and informal atmosphere. The instruments played would be loud - bagpipes, percussion and shawms. At Maytime, a closed ring of men and women would dance around a central point, which might be a Maypole, festooned in streamers held by the dancers. This represented the Devil caught up in chains and imprisoned by the dancing ring of people.

Morris Dancers Morris dancers would appear at fairs and gatherings, performing intricate dances, sometimes using sticks or swords which represented the weapons carried into battle against Saracens during the Crusades. In fact, it is believed the word *morris* derives from *Moorish*.

Music of the Castle

In the Great Hall of the castle, one could find food, gambling, dancing, singing, storytelling and other forms of entertainment. There might be a *minstrel's gallery,* or small balcony, overlooking the banquet hall and providing out-of-the-way space where the musicians could play. *(See illustration on page 64)*

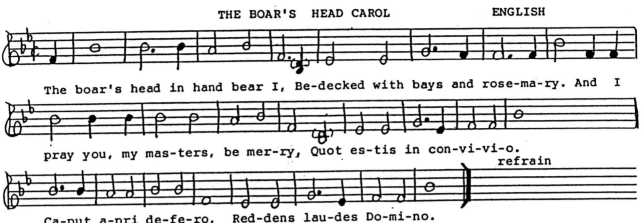

THE BOAR'S HEAD CAROL   ENGLISH

The boar's head in hand bear I, Be-decked with bays and rose-ma-ry. And I

pray you, my mas-ters, be mer-ry, Quot es-tis in con-vi-vi-o.

                                                            refrain

Ca-put a-pri de-fe-ro, Red-dens lau-des Do-mi-no.

2. The boar's head, as I understand,
   Is the bravest dish in all the land.
   When thus bedecked with a gay garland,
   Let us servire cantico.
                                   Refrain

3. Our steward hath provided this
   In honor of the King of Bliss.
   Which on this day to be served is,
   In reginensi Atrio.
                                   Refrain

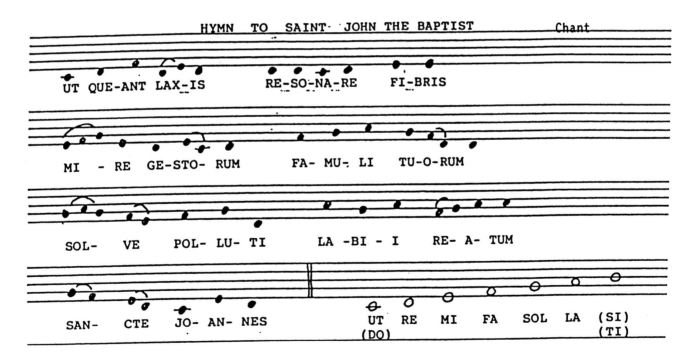

HYMN TO SAINT JOHN THE BAPTIST   Chant

UT QUE-ANT LAX-IS   RE-SO-NA-RE   FI-BRIS

MI - RE GE-STO- RUM   FA- MU- LI   TU-O-RUM

SOL- VE POL- LU- TI   LA -BI - I   RE- A- TUM

SAN- CTE JO- AN- NES   UT RE MI FA SOL LA (SI)
                            (DO)   (TI)

Translation: That thy servants may freely sing forth the wonders of thy deeds, remove all stain of guilt from their unclean lips, O Saint John.

Minstrels and Troubadours Minstrels and troubadours were welcomed into the court. These singers made their livings by entertaining at manor houses and castles. They were able to tell stories of battles and heroic deeds. They carried news and gossip to many corners of the land. In an age without television and radio they provided information as well as entertainment. Other itinerant entertainers such as jugglers and acrobats were welcomed also. These traveling entertainers were on a very low rung of the social hierarchy. It was not until the minstrels developed guilds that they were able to attain any status in society.

By the thirteenth century, it had become fashionable for a knight to be a musician and poet. The concept of courtly love-songs and poetry written to a lady came into vogue. Music was a part of the life of a knight from an early age. When a young boy was sent to be a page in the service of the lady of a castle, he was expected to learn courtesy and gracious airs. He was taught music by tutors along with other subjects.

Music was part of the knight's investiture ceremony, fanfares played on trumpets and drums announced knights at a joust, marches were played for processions. Music had a role in war. The steady beat of the drums kept armies marching together, the trumpets heralded the arrival of new troops and loud instruments were used by military bands to instill fear in the enemy.

King Richard the Lionheart Richard I, called Lionheart, King of England from 1189-1199, led the Third Crusade against Saladin. Richard was a good musician and composed many songs which he performed in the style of the minstrels. Upon returning from the Crusades, Richard was taken captive in the castle of Duernstein. According to legend, his squire, Blondel de Nesle, sought long and hard for his king. One day he heard a voice singing a familiar tune. It was Richard. Blondel was able to set him free because of hearing his king's music.

Ars Nova Music of the fourteenth century is known as the *Ars Nova*, or New Art. Just as the decline of feudal aristocracy and the weakening of the church's authority are taking place, change and diversity are occurring in the music. Monophonic (one-voice) music was being replaced by polyphonic (many-voiced) music, with greater rhythmic and metrical freedom as well as more frequent use of thirds and sixths as harmonic intervals.

The *cantus firmus* or *main melody* was no longer written in the tenor line. The word *tenor* comes from the French verb *tenir* which means to hold, because the tenor had to hold on to the melody. Now the melody was given to the top line, known as the *superius* (soprano), and the *altus* (alto) was written *higher* than the tenor line. A lower part was added beneath the tenor, called the *bassus* (bass), or foundation of the chord. These became the norms for part-writing, and opened the door to the secular polyphonic madrigals of the Renaissance.

Musicians of the Fifteenth Century Music, art and literature flourished in the Burgundian courts of Duke Philip the Good (1419-1467) and Charles the Bold (1467-77). Famous composers of the fifteenth century include John Dunstable (1370?-1453), Roy Henry - who was probably Henry V (1387-1422), Josquin des Pres (1450?-1521), Heinrich Isaac (1450?-1517), Guillaume Dufy (1400?-1474), Jacob Obrecht (1450-1505) and Johannes Ockhegem (1430?-1495). Recordings of many of these composers' works are available in public libraries.

Dances of the Middle Ages

Line and Circle Dances Two types of dances were performed during the Middle Ages: line dances such as the *farandole* and the *estampie*, and circle dances, often called *round* dances, like the *bransle* (pronounced brawl) and *carole*. Peasants and aristocrats performed the same dances, but in different settings. The wealthy danced indoors at banquets and feasts, while peasants danced at outdoor celebrations. Of course, the clergy frowned upon such activities and associated dancing with the devil.

Outdoor dancing required louder instruments such as the *crumhorn, shawm, sackbut* and horn. Indoor dances were accompanied by softer instruments such as recorders, lutes, harps and *psaltery*.

Some dances were very sedate. In the *Pavane*, each couple would follow one another around the perimeter of the room while walking in time to the music. Some dances, such as the *farandole*, lost their popularity because of a change in fashion. When the hennin, the tall pointed hat of the fifteenth century, became fashionable, ladies found it too difficult to dance the farandole while balancing a hennin on their heads. In this case, fashion won and the dance became unpopular. The French names of many dances remind us that it was French-speaking aristocrats who shaped English culture in the later Middle Ages.

Line Dances

Thread the Needle All stand in a line with hands joined. The leader and second in line form a one-handed arch through which the rest of the line passes. When all are through, a new arch is formed at the beginning of the line by the next two.

L'Escargot The name of this dance (pronounced les-car-go) means *snail* in French, because its spiral shape is reminiscent of a snail's shell. The leader leads the line around in a spiral, followed by the second in line until the line is wound into a tight spiral. The person on the outer end begins to unwind the snail's shell.

Estampie This name (pronounced es-tam-pee) means *stamp* in French. Dancers form a line with hands joined at waist level. Turn body to the left while face is turned towards front. Steps are taken forward and backward on the strong beat; move forward with little steps, and backward with smaller steps:

> Left — step forward,
> Right — step back.
> Left, right, left — in place;
> Stamp with right.

> Right — step forward,
> Left — step back.
> Right, left, right — in place;
> Stamp with left.

> Hint: the foot which stamps will lead off on the next step.
> Use lots of energy, bend knees on first step. Stay up on toes.

Circle Dances

The Bransle Named from the French word *branler* (pronounced brawl), to sway, these dances were performed in stepping circles with various combinations of stepping together either in a single step or a double step. The dancers would move first in one direction, then back in the other direction.

The Washerwoman's Bransle (see music on next page)

Stand with partner in circle.
Step to left, bring right foot to left. Repeat.
Step to right, bring left foot to right. Repeat.
Repeat entire sequence.
Women shake index fingers reprovingly at men
. . . who nonchalantly place hands on hips.
Reverse roles on repeat.
Step to left, bring right foot to left.
Repeat but add a clap at end.
Step to right, bring left foot to right. Repeat.
Step to left, bring right foot to left.
Repeat but add a clap at end.
Turn in place and jump on final chord.

The manuscript of **Sumer is icumen in**,
discovered near Reading, England, circa 1240,
is a famous example of a *round*.

Activities and vocabulary words after music ➡

WASHERWOMAN'S BRANSLE

Arbeau

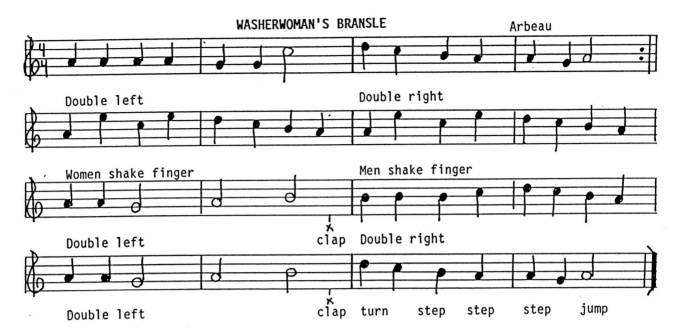

Double left   Double right

Women shake finger   Men shake finger

Double left   clap Double right

Double left   clap turn step step step jump

This bransle is performed in a circle with hands joined. Partners turn and face each other when shaking their fingers; the other partner places hands on hips. The jump at the end is for men to show off. The higher the jump, the more virile the man!

```
double left                 (step together to left-2 times)
double right                (step together to right-2 times)
repeat entire sequence above
women shake right index finger at partner; men place hands on hips
men shake right index finger at partner; women place hands on hips
double left then clap, double right
double left then clap, make a turn to right
step in a circle three times then men jump
```

The clapping is supposed to signify the sound of washerwomen in Paris as they slap clothes against the rocks in the Seine in an effort to clean the clothes.

A KNIGHT TO REMEMBER

The fair lady,   , asked the handsome knight, Sir

to carry her   of honor into the joust. He agreed,

for the lady was beautiful! He hoped to win, else he would end up

with   on his   . As Sir

waited for the tournament to begin, he paced his tent like a

lion. He was very nervous. "If I lose, I'll never   able

to   Lady   again!" he thought.

Soon it was time for the joust to begin. Sir   came

up to Sir   and began to make fun of him, saying, "I'll

smash your   ! You will

be ____ !" Sir ____ calmly suggested

that they make a friendly wager on the outcome of the fight. "Sir

____ , I will give you the ____ to my

castle if you win, but if I win, you must give me a precious

a jewel like a diamond!"

"I agree," said Sir ____ . "Let's fight!" They

soon were charging at each other from horseback. Sir

knocked Sir ____ to the ground and stood over him with

his sword drawn. "No! I ____ for mercy!" cried Sir

And he received it.   THE END.

OATS AND BEANS

Traditional

Oats and beans and bar-ley grow, Oats and beans and bar-ley grow

Do you or I or a-ny-one know, how oats and beans and bar-ley grow?

1. First the farmer plants the seed   (bend over and plant seed)
   Stands up tall and takes his ease   (stand and stretch)
   Stamps his feet and claps his hands   (do appropriate actions)
   And turns around to view his land.   (turn and shade eyes with hand)
   Chorus
2. Then the farmer waters the ground   (water with watering can)
   Watches the sun shine all around   (look up and shade eyes)
   Stamps his feet and claps his hands   (do appropriate actions)
   And turns around to view his land.   (turn and shade eyes with hand)
   Chorus

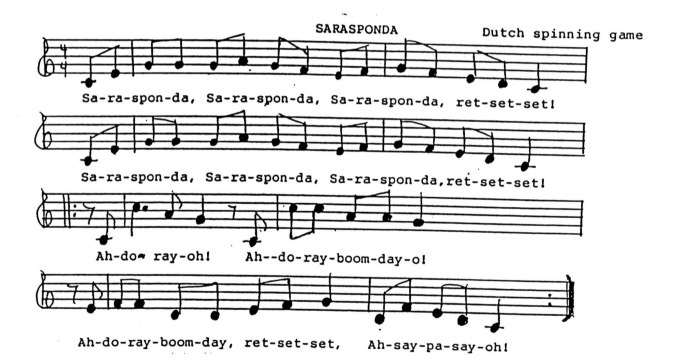

SARASPONDA

Dutch spinning game

Sa-ra-spon-da, Sa-ra-spon-da, Sa-ra-spon-da, ret-set-set!

Sa-ra-spon-da, Sa-ra-spon-da, Sa-ra-spon-da, ret-set-set!

Ah-do ray-oh! Ah--do-ray-boom-day-o!

Ah-do-ray-boom-day, ret-set-set, Ah-say-pa-say-oh!

(Song increases in tempo with each repetition).

Activities

9-1. Peddlers' Street Cries

Pretend you are a merchant in a medieval marketplace. Cry out in a sing-song voice to attract attention to your wares. Make up a short description of your wares:

> Herbs! Healthy herbs!
> Who'll buy my fresh fish!
> Spices, fragrant spices!
> Gems from afar!

Move around and interact with other merchants and customers.

9-2. Troubadour Song

Write a song in the style of a fifteenth-century troubadour.
What would his subject be? Who are the characters?
In what country, and at what date does it take place?
If the song tells a story, decide on the plot.
Do any lines rhyme?
How is the song to be performed?
Will you use any instruments?

9-3. Music Puzzle - *A Knight to Remember*

Fill in the spaces in the words to this song. Remember, every line of the staff in the treble clef has a letter name: E,G,B,D,F; and every space on the staff has a letter name too: F,A,C,E. Using these note names, figure out the missing words.

9-4. Create a Medieval Music Manuscript

Rewrite a familiar song using shape notes. Do not use any bar lines. Replace the note values of today with the appropriate shaped note from the Middle Ages:

	Notes c. 1425	Notes near end of 16th century	Present day notation	
brevis				breve = 8 beats
semibrevis				whole = 4 beats
minima				half = 2 beats
semimima				quarter = 1 beat

Unfilled notes, common around 1425, were drawn that way to save ink.
Diamond and square-shaped notes changed to rounded notes near the end of the 16th century.

More activities & vocabulary words ➡

9-5. Learn an Old Song

Some of the old round songs and carols we all know are hundreds of years old or are similar to very old songs. Divide the class in parts, and sing *Row, row, row your boat; Frere Jacques; Sur le pont d'Avignon; Hickory, Dickory Dock; etc. Greensleaves* is another old song that is widely known.

Vocabulary Words for Chapter Nine

Gregorian chant
plain-song
plain-chants
polyphony
troping
troubadour
minstrel
maypole
morris dancers
minstrel's gallery
farandole
estampie
bransle
carole
crumhorn
sackbut
shawm
psaltery

Chapter Ten

Art and Artists

Early Medieval Art

Religious Art Most art produced in the Middle Ages was *religious*. It was made for the glory of God, to teach people about their religion, and to inspire them with a sense of the wonders of heaven and the horrors of hell.

Jewish, Islamic, and in some periods Byzantine Christian theologians objected to the creation of images of people, on the grounds that only God should make men, but western Christianity never developed this prohibition, and used all kinds of images to teach an illiterate population the stories and beliefs of their religion.

Symbolism Early medieval art was *symbolic*: the images it portrayed stood for something outside themselves, and conveyed ideas and beliefs to the onlookers who knew how to interpret these symbols. For example, everyone knew that the symbols for the four Evangelists, the apostles who wrote the gospels, were a lion for St. Mark, an eagle for St. John, an ox for St. Luke, and a winged man for St. Matthew.

Celtic, Anglo-Saxon and Viking Art Early medieval art was *decorative*, not realistic. In northern Europe, artists wove intricate patterns of colored lines, called *interlacing*, which aimed to delight the eye rather than to convey an illusion of reality.

In writing, the interlaced line winds and spirals on, circling around the letter or even the whole page, doubling back and often ending in an animal's head. Sometimes the animal bites his own tail, and part of the line may form long thin legs to complete the beast.

This same kind of linear pattern is found on stone carvings, such as the Irish High Crosses; on metalwork such as jewelry, as in the Anglo-Saxon Sutton Hoo hoard; and on wooden objects such as Viking boats, whose prow is often a sleek animal head.

Illuminated Manuscripts Medieval books are called *manuscripts,* which means written by hand. Sometimes the *scribes* who wrote them also painted the decorations and pictures in them, but more often this was done by specialists called *illuminators,* because they brightened the page with gorgeous colored ink, paint, and even gold and silver. The painters of early illuminated manuscripts aimed to produce a beautiful flat page, they did not try to produce an illusion of three-dimensional space.

Irish and Hiberno-Saxon Manuscripts Illuminators drew borders around the text, and pictures in the text, but they also transformed the letters themselves into pictures. The capital letters in some early medieval illuminated manuscripts become almost illegible because they are so elaborated with ornament and picture. Some Irish monastic books are considered among the most beautiful works of medieval art: two gospel books, the *Book of Kells* (circa 800) and the *Book of Durrow* (circa 650) are among the most famous. The *Lindisfarne Gospels* was another beautiful monastic book made in Northumbria, England, in about A.D. 700. Manuscripts like these were extremely rare and valuable: to give them the most brilliant color possible, inks to decorate them were made from real gold and silver, and crushed lapis lazuli. *(See illustrations in this chapter)*

Parchment and Vellum Medieval manuscripts were written on *parchment* or *vellum*, fine leather from sheep or calf-skin. Six or eight thin semi-translucent pieces of leather were piled up, and stitched down the middle to make a *gathering*. They were then folded along the stitching, and several gatherings were sewn together to make a book, which was then bound in heavier leather. Paper had been invented in China in ancient times, but was not known in Europe until the twelfth century, and was still very unusual until the fifteenth century. Ink was made from lampblack (soot) and oak gall, and writing was done with a quill pen.

Panel Painting and Fresco Paintings were also done on wooden panels covered with a thin coat of plaster called *gesso*. Powdered pigments were used, mixed with egg yolk. Byzantine *icons* were painted in this medium: an icon is a religious painting in traditional East European style. A master of panel painting was the early fourteenth-century *Duccio di Buoninsegna* (pronounced Doo-cho dee Bwone-in-sen-ya) whose magnificent altarpiece, the *Maiesta* (Majesty) is preserved in the cathedral of Siena, Italy.

Another type of medieval painting was *fresco*, which was watercolor painting on wet plaster. This was often used for wall paintings, notably by *Giotto* (pronounced Jot-toe, 1266?-1337?) at the church of San Francesco in Assisi and the Arena Chapel in Padua, Italy. *Ambrogio Lorenzetti* (died 1348?) painted a magnificent fresco, the *Allegory of Good and Bad Government* in the Town Hall of Siena in 1337-39.

Later Medieval Art

Later medieval art was both *symbolic* and *narrative* or *pictorial*. It was *symbolic* because it continued to use one image to represent another: an ox could still represent the Evangelist Luke, for example; and it was *narrative* or *pictorial* because it also used straightforward representation of images to tell a story: a scene of a peasant plowing with an ox might tell a simple story of farm labors. Stories from the bible and saints' lives were represented all over churches, starting at the sculptured scenes decorating entrance porches and doorways, and including stained glass windows, sculpture on columns and pulpits, and painted or mosaic walls and ceilings.

Romanesque Art The two great original styles of later medieval art were *romanesque* and *gothic*. Romanesque art and architecture flourished from about A.D. 1000–1200, and is so called because it resembles the architecture of ancient Rome. It is characterized by round arches, *barrel vaults* (vaulting is heavy stone roofing — see the illustration), massive walls with small round-arched windows, heavy columns decorated with fantastic sculptured humans, animals and monsters writhing in grotesque patterns all over the available space. Romanesque painting shows a similar fondness for the fantastic and grotesque, and a similar desire to push against the boundaries of available space.

Gothic Art Gothic art began near Paris, in the monastic church of St.-Denis, and spread from there through France and beyond. Gothic art flourished from about A.D. 1150 to the end of the Middle Ages. It was characterized in architecture by tall spires, *ribbed groined vaulting,* pointed arches, slender elongated columns, walls pierced by huge stained glass windows, supported from outside the building by *flying buttresses* of stone, invisible from within *(see illustrations of vaulting and buttresses, next pages)*.

Gothic Art continued ➡

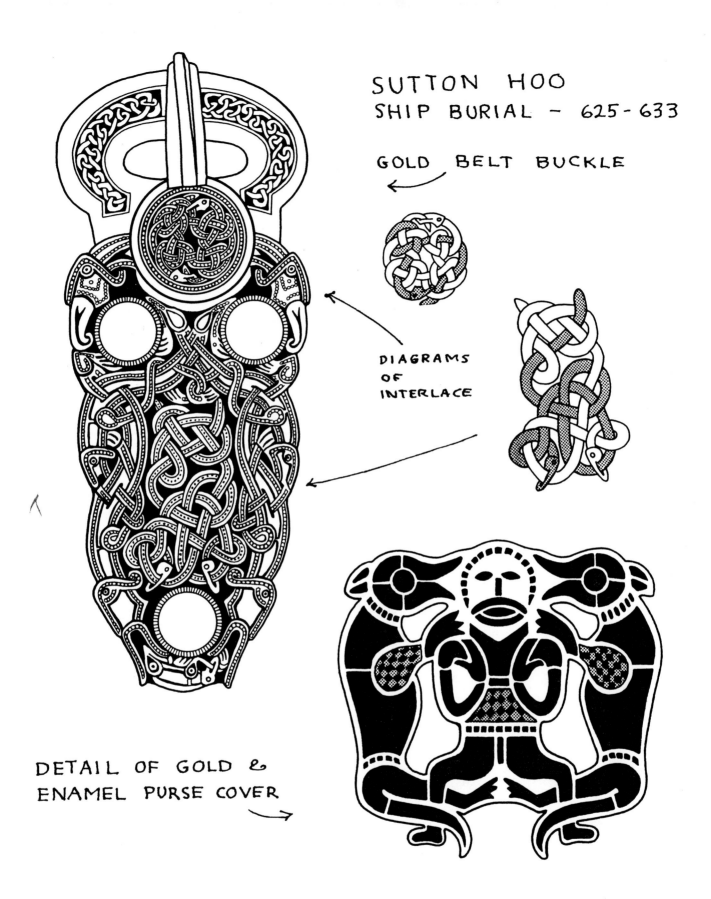

SUTTON HOO
SHIP BURIAL — 625 - 633

GOLD BELT BUCKLE

DIAGRAMS
OF
INTERLACE

DETAIL OF GOLD &
ENAMEL PURSE COVER →

VIKING AGE

STONE CROSS   NORTH OF ENGLAND   10ᵀᴴ CENTURY

BOOK OF KELLS
DECORATED INITIAL
T

DECORATIONS FROM THE BOOK OF DURROW 7ᵀᴴ CENTURY

SPIRAL PATTERN

ANIMAL INTERLACE

LION FROM THE BOOK OF LINDISFARNE

ROMANESQUE AND GOTHIC ARCHITECTURE

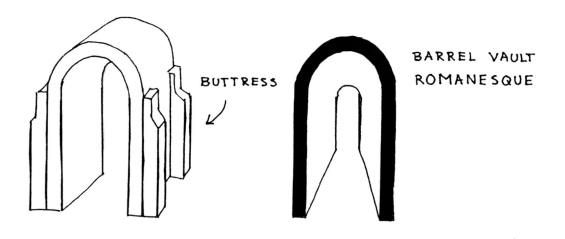

BUTTRESS

BARREL VAULT
ROMANESQUE

ROMANESQUE

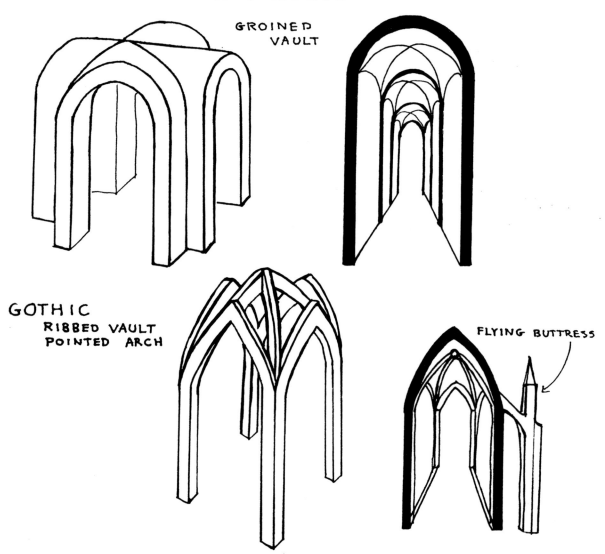

GROINED
VAULT

GOTHIC
RIBBED VAULT
POINTED ARCH

FLYING BUTTRESS

FLYING BUTTRESS BASED ON A DRAWING
BY VILLARD DE HONNECOURT - 13TH CENTURY

Picture the Middle Ages page 74h

The massiveness of romanesque changed into the tall slender spaces of the great gothic cathedrals, light-filled and colorful. The grotesque was replaced by gentle paintings and sculpture of graceful swaying figures, their faces and gestures expressing human emotions in a lifelike way never before achieved.

The fifteenth-century wooden statue of St. George and the Dragon *(see photo on lefthand page)* exemplifies the gentleness and elegance of gothic sculpture, while other illustrations exemplify various periods of gothic book illustration. The illustration of *Monastic Life* on page **42a** represents late thirteenth-century styles, with its scenes confined tightly within the frame, while *On the Manor* on page **50** represents mid-fourteenth-century illumination with its delicate vine ornament with small scenes intertwined. *Merchants and Trades of the Town* on page **22a**, and *A Banquet in the Castle* on page **52a** represent fifteenth-century styles, with their heavily pictorial borders, which have in effect become another picture.

Architects and Architecture The twelfth and thirteenth centuries were a great age for architecture, with cathedrals and monastic churches constructed and renovated all over Europe. Towns took great pride in their churches, and regarded a handsome large structure as a necessary expression of their piety and prosperity.

Despite their number and importance, we know the names of very few architects from the period. The great *Abbot Suger* (1081-1151) is known to us more through his importance in the politics of his age than for his architectural importance as the builder of the first gothic cathedral at St.-Denis, near Paris. One of the few gothic architects whose name we know is *Villard de Honnnecourt* (pronounced Vee-yard Don-eh-coor), who traveled to study existing buildings and drew what he saw in a model book, circa 1230-40. Villard was also interested in machines, and drew many examples both real and fantastic. Unfortunately, we do not know of any actual buildings designed by him.

Cathedrals Building a cathedral was a huge undertaking that frequently took all the resources of the town concerned for several generations. It was standard for the builders to run out of money before the building was complete. They would then put a temporary roof on the part of the structure that was usable, and hold services in it until they could proceed with their building campaigns. The length of time involved explains why so many gothic churches look unfinished, with only one instead of two towers flanking the west entrance, or with two unmatching towers — one built a generation or more after the other, and each of them reflecting the latest taste in architecture at the time it was built.

Stained Glass Stained glass, a major medieval artistic development, was a product of the technique of coloring glass with metallic oxides to produce glowing colors. Lines were also painted on the glass, for example to indicate facial features. Stained glass had been made in the Near East from the days of ancient Rome, but its use was greatly expanded and its full potential realized in the gothic architecture of the 12th and 13th centuries. Gothic architects and designers from Abbot Suger on believed the glowing colors of stained glass infused a church interior with a semblance of the luminous brilliance of paradise. Tracery, the stone frame surrounding the window, was shaped in graceful floral circles called *rose windows,* or in tall narrow vertical windows terminating in a gothic arch.

The program of decoration for each church was carefully planned to tell all the major religious stories and beliefs. The stained glass windows that lighted gothic churches were called the *biblia pauperum* (pronounced bib-lee-ah pow-per-oom), or *bibles of the poor*, because they told major stories from the bible in glowing colors and beautiful patterns for the illiterate masses. Since everyone went to church on Sunday, and on many holy days (which gave us the word *holiday*), there was plenty of opportunity to learn the bible stories and saints' lives.

Guilds and Art Major *guilds*, the early trade unions, paid for windows in many cathedrals, and often included small scenes of their members at work around the central image of a biblical event. At Chartres Cathedral near Paris, several guilds paid for the windows. The cordwainers' (shoemakers) guild, for example, supplied a great window showing the Death of Mary, Christ's mother, with small scenes underneath it showing their own members choosing and cutting leather, and making shoes. *(A full-size facsimile may be seen in the Higgins Armory Museum in Worcester, Massachusetts.)* Thus guilds attested to their members' importance in the community, and their charitable contributions.

Portraits Medieval people did not regularly have their portraits painted during their lives: such individual glorification was regarded as impious. But just as the guilds wanted to see themselves in the windows at Chartres, so aristocratic families who built churches or donated glass or sculpture, or commissioned illuminated manuscripts, wanted to see themselves commemorated. Portraits of donors were a common element in medieval art: wealthy patrons are shown piously on their knees before the heavenly personage to whom the work is dedicated, an acceptable way of honoring the donor along with the divine. Important people were also memorialized in their tombs, which often included portraits of the deceased sculpted in stone or incised in brass or enamel.

Humor Despite its serious religious purpose, *humor* is found throughout medieval art. Even the most serious religious manuscripts may have *drolleries* in the margins, small humorous scenes of human and animal playfulness, and sculptures on church doorways and monastic cloister columns often include entertaining episodes. A twelfth-century Cistercian theological manuscript *(Moralia in Job)* shows a humorous gardening scene, with a man high in a tree pruning its branches, unaware of the monk at the foot of the tree who is chopping it down.

Museum Resources Many American and European museums display medieval art. The Cloisters, a branch of the Metropolitan Museum of Art at Fort Tryon Park, New York City, is completely devoted to all aspects of medieval art. The Higgins Armory Museum in Worcester, Massachusetts, is the only museum in the Americas solely dedicated to arms and armor, and has a thrilling display of armored knights in a gothic Great Hall.

NOTRE DAME PARIS
ROSE WINDOW NORTH TRANSEPT

Picture the Middle Ages page 76a

NOTRE DAME - PARIS

ROSE WINDOW

TRACERY PATTERNS

Goudy Text

ABCDEFGHIJ
KLMNOPQ
RSTUVW
XYZ

abcdefghijklmnopqrs
tuvwxyz
1234567890 $&!?

CELTIC ALPHABET

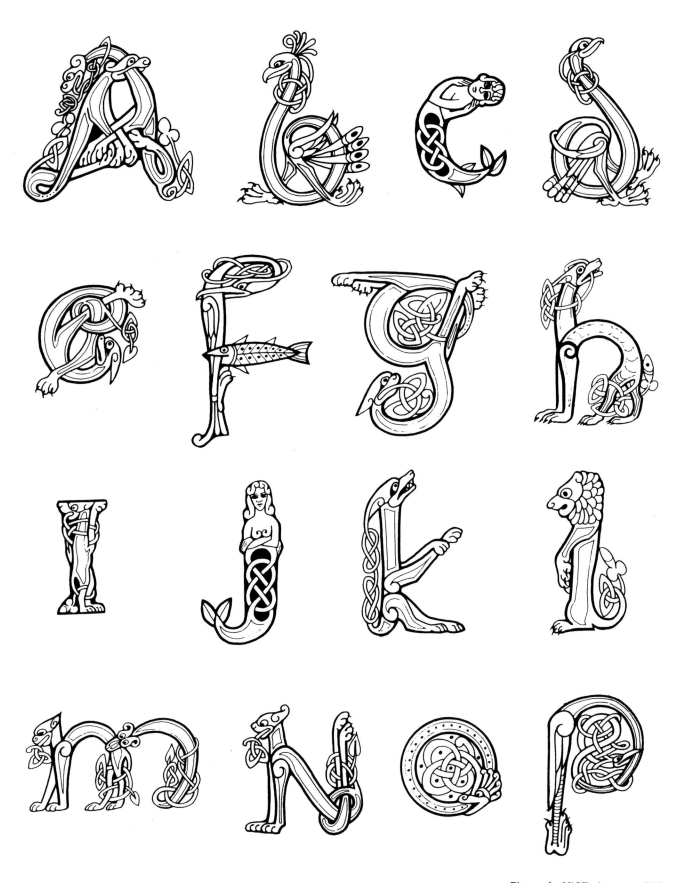

CELTIC ALPHABET

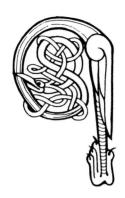 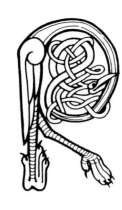  

PAPER BAG (OR BOX) CASTLE

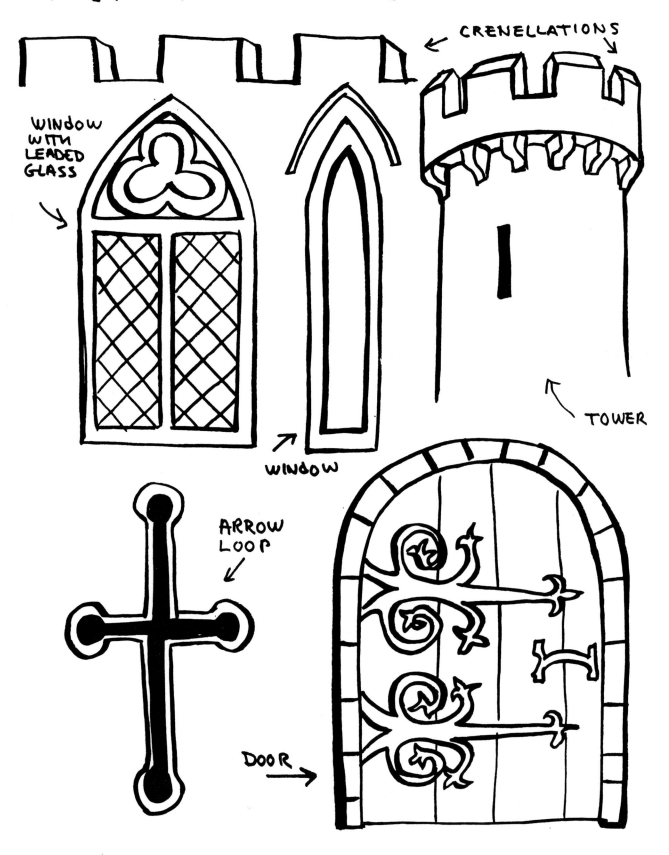

CRENELLATIONS

WINDOW WITH LEADED GLASS

TOWER

WINDOW

ARROW LOOP

DOOR

Activities

Architecture and Sculpture

10-1. Grocery Bag Castles

A clean brown paper grocery bag is shaped like many castles, tall and straight. Cut towers on the top. On scrap paper, trace and cut out the battlements, doors, and other elements drawn here, and glue them on. Paint the bag, then use it to hold your medieval projects!

10-2. Cardboard Box Castles

The drawings here can also be used to decorate three-dimensional castles made from boxes. Rectangular sugar and rice boxes, and round oat-meal boxes or coffee cans covered with paper, can be assembled on a corrugated cardboard base to make a complex late-medieval castle, with several towers and entrances. Make roofs for the round towers by folding construction paper into a cone. Add flags on tooth-picks to the towers. Paint the landscape around your castle. Is it surrounded by a moat, or a dry ditch? Has it access to water, farmland, firewood? Is it placed protectively on a cliff or mountain top?

10-3. Monstrous Gargoyles

Gargoyles are the waterspouts that project from the roofs of medieval churches, ending in an animal or monster head with open mouth to let the rain flow out. Make one or two gargoyles from self-hardening clay. They may be *dragons* or other medieval monsters: *griffins* or *gryphons* — beasts with an eagle's head and wings and a lion's body, or *wyverns* — serpents with twisting tails, two front legs and a dragon's head. Indent a depression on the central top back with your finger, so they can hang up. Or make them with a flat bottom and back, to use as bookends. Paint them in a stony color when dry.

10-4. Mirrors

Medieval mirrors were made from highly-polished metal, not glass, with beautifully-carved ivory backs. Make yours 6 inches square or round, from foil-covered cardboard. Cover the back and edges of the mirror with a low relief sculptured plaque made from self-hardening clay. Paint the mirror when dry. In the Middle Ages, mirrors were popular gifts for Valentine's Day.

Calligraphy and Illumination

10-5. Illuminated Initial *(See the Celtic Interlace and Gothic Alphabets on lefthand pages)*

Write out a poem or short story, or an invitation to a medieval banquet or tournament, in a medieval script. Illuminate the initial letter of each paragraph in a medieval style, either decorative or pictorial. Enclose the text in a decorative border.

10-6. Printed Initial

In the late 15th century when printed books were still new, printers sometimes enlivened the printed text page with a mix of printed and hand-drawn initial letters. Cut your initial in reverse on an eraser, ink and print it, and draw a design around it.

Stained Glass

10-7. Storied Windows

The stone surround which defines a stained glass window is called its *tracery*. Within the tracery, the window is held together by a lead *armature* which separates the different colored pieces of glass. Using the examples of tracery illustrated in this chapter, design your own window to tell a medieval story. Either color it with markers or paint, or cut your design from transparent plastic gels. Paint black lines on your colored glass to define faces and other details. Punch a hole at the top and hang in a window.

10-8. Heraldic Glass

Draw and color a coat-of-arms on paper in stained glass style, with bold black lines indicating the armature. Take a piece of clear window glass and cover all its edges with colored tape. Place it over your drawing and copy the design with paint. Tie cord around it and hang it in a window.

10-9. Stained Glass Cookies

Make a batch of sugar cookie dough. Chill for several hours, then roll out on a floured surface into several thin ropes about one quarter inch thick. Shape the ropes into window traceries on a foil-covered baking sheet. Take two packages of lollipops or fruit candy and crush each color separately. Fill cookie windows with different colored candies and bake at 350 degrees for 5 minutes or until candy is melted. Make a hole in the top center of each window with a cake tester so candies may be hung. Cool completely before removing from baking sheet.

Tapestry

10-10. Bayeux Updated

Using the Bayeux Tapestry *(see page 54)* as a model, choose a story to tell. The story could be about King Arthur and his court, Robin Hood and his band, or even about something much more modern. Break the story down into small elements, and assign each element to one or two students. Paint and write the story on pieces cut from a roll of craft paper 2 feet wide, the same size as the original, then assemble and hang in the classroom or corridor.

10-11. Class Tapestry Banner Project

Either: Decide on a story about a medieval character — King Arthur, Charlemagne, Joan of Arc, Eleanor of Aquitaine. The students work in teams of two; each team chooses one incident from the story and illustrates it on a 9 x 11 inch piece of burlap, felt or old fabric, using thread to outline the picture, or appliqued fabric scraps, stitched or glued on. The pictures may be assembled on a cotton banner cut from one and a quarter yards of 42 inch wide fabric, hung from 5 x 4 inch long tabs made from 4 feet of braid. A white felt panel is hung on the back of the banner, and signed in marker with the date and each student's name, to make a permanent record of the unit for the home-room.

Or: Make the same story-telling banner, but use incidents from the class' experience as the basis of the pictures — field-trips, successful games, new subjects studied, a special teacher, books read, etc.

Vocabulary Words for Chapter Ten

interlacing	pictorial art	rose window
illuminated manuscripts	romanesque art	biblia pauperum
illuminators	gothic art	cordwainers
vellum	barrel vaults	drolleries
gathering	vaulting	gargoyles
gesso	grotesque	griffins
fresco	groined vaulting	wyverns
altarpiece	flying buttresses	symbolism
narrative art	stained glass	

Medieval Art and Artists Word Search

The words run forwards, backwards, up and down!

M	A	N	U	S	C	R	I	P	T
E	N	S	Y	M	B	O	L	Z	V
R	O	M	A	N	E	S	Q	U	E
U	T	C	O	C	S	E	R	F	L
T	T	I	N	S	P	W	C	A	L
P	O	H	O	U	I	I	R	N	U
L	I	T	R	G	R	N	O	G	M
U	G	O	T	E	E	D	T	E	X
C	Y	G	A	R	G	O	Y	L	E
S	H	A	P	E	D	W	O	O	D

Word List

Angel .... heavenly spirit
Fresco .... painting made on wet plaster
Gargoyle .... cathedral water-spout shaped like a monster
Giotto .... medieval Italian painter
Gothic .... style of medieval art and architecture
Manuscript .... book written by hand
Patron .... person who commissions art work
Romanesque .... style preceding Gothic in medieval art
Rose window .... round stained glass window
Sculpture .... three-dimensional art
Shaped wood .... wood carved in decorative patterns
Spire .... tall thin projection above church tower
Suger .... famous French monk
Symbol .... thing which stands for something else
Torc .... stiff round metal necklace or bracelet
Vellum .... calf skin used for writing on

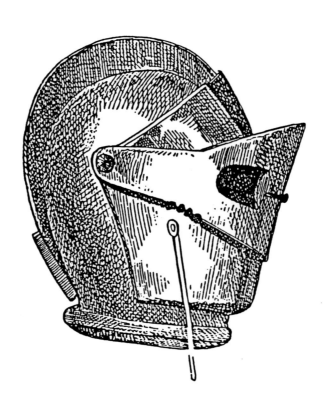

Chapter Eleven

Medieval Literature

Medieval people loved stories. Bible stories and stories about the saints and the miracles they performed were told to them in church each Sunday and holy day. Grandmothers caring for children told them stories about strange and wonderful things that had happened when they were young — *old wives' tales.*

Since most people could not read, stories were read aloud, or sung or told after dinner. Ladies in castles liked to listen to someone reading aloud as they worked on their needlework. Even in monasteries, monks and nuns listened to improving stories about the saints as they ate dinner in silence. Many stories were in verse form, because the rhyme and rhythm helped people to remember the thousands of lines in a *romance*, the name given to a long story about heroes and heroines, King Arthur or Helen of Troy.

Caedmon, the Earliest English Poet

Professional poets and musicians called *minstrels* or *troubadours* traveled from castle to castle, bringing new tales and songs to entertain the lord and his guests after dinner. Ordinary people were also expected to entertain the company at the end of the meal. A touching story from England tells of a shepherd called Caedmon (pronounced Cad-mon) who lived in the seventh century at the monastery of Whitby, a double monastery containing a household of monks and a separate household of nuns, which was ruled by a famous abbess, St. Hilda.

At the end of dinner one evening, the harp was being passed around among the diners and each one was expected to sing something. Poor Caedmon could not sing, so he left the hall and went back to his stable to sleep with his flock. As he slept, he dreamt an angel came to him, and ordered him to sing something. "I cannot," he replied, but the angel said, "Sing of the Creation."

In his dream, Caedmon immediately sang a song in Old English verse, telling of God's creation of the world. Next morning, he went to the Abbess Hilda and her counselors and told them his dream. They questioned him to discover if his visitor were angelic or demonic, and decided it was a true messenger from God. Hilda urged Caedmon to become a monk, which he did, and composed many more songs. The great historian Bede (672-735) wrote Caedmon's story and preserved his name, making him the earliest English poet known to us.

Medieval Language

Caedmon's language was what we call *Old English* or *Anglo-Saxon*, the language brought to England by the Angles, Saxons and other Germanic tribes who moved there in the fifth and sixth centuries. It is very different from the modern English we speak. The first line of Caedmon's song is:

> *Nu scylan hergan*   *hefaenricaes uard*
> Now we must praise   the heavenly ward

Many other Old English poems are preserved, but we do not know who composed them. The most famous is *Beowulf* (pronounced Bay-oh-wolf), a tragic tale of the heroic Beowulf's life and defeat of the evil monster Grendel and his mother, dating from the eighth century but written down in the tenth.

Old English was spoken in England until the eleventh century, when Duke William and his French-speaking knights invaded from Normandy and conquered the country at the Battle of Hastings in 1066. For the next two centuries, the kings and lords of England spoke French, while the peasants and poor craftsmen spoke an English that was being changed by the addition of many French words.

An English herdsman like Caedmon tended his *cattle*, while the Norman lady in the castle consulted her cook about the roasting of her *beef*, from the French *boeuf*. Similarly, the English shepherdess cared for her *sheep*, but the French baron ordered *mutton* (from the French *mouton*) for dinner.

Norman knights and barons wore armor, so in English we call armor parts by French names: *sabatons* for armored shoes, *gorget* for neck defence, *gauntlets* for armored gloves. (So *to throw down the gauntlet* came to mean, *to challenge someone to a duel*.)

While the aristocrats in the castle were speaking French, the learned monks and scholars of the church spoke Latin, and that became the international language of universities and diplomats. So many Latin words came into English, and are still used today, for example, circus, senator and forum.

Gradually the French and English intermarried, and aristocrats began speaking English, but an English enriched by French influence and vocabulary. By the fourteenth century when Geoffrey Chaucer (1343?-1400) was writing, Old English had become *Middle English* and was much closer to our modern language.

The first lines of Chaucer's *Canterbury Tales* are quite easy to understand:

> *Whan that Aprill with his shoures soote*
> *The droghte of March hath perced to the roote*
> "When April with its sweet showers
> The drought of March has pierced to the root."

Middle English changed to modern English at the end of the fifteenth century, when the Middle Ages was also ending. The great factor influencing language at the time was Gutenberg's invention of printing with movable type, which made books available to far more people than ever before, encouraged the spread of reading and writing, and contributed to a standardization of language.

Types of Medieval Literature

Riddles Popular in many languages, including Old Irish, Old English and Old Norse. Here are some translated adaptations from Old English. (Old English verse is written in two half-lines, joined by alliteration, not rhyme. Each half-line has two stresses. Any vowel alliterates with any other vowel. Alliteration is often imperfect.)

What Am I?

Alone am I	war-weary
sword slashed	endlessly attacked.
No doctor's cure	or herbal healing
succors me,	but smith's strike
hammer's hurt	endless battle.

(Answer: a shield)

Who Am I?

I humbly slither	through stories and tales.
Not understanding	I am still nourished.
My wings take flight	from a poet's fancy.
My dining destructive,	my dessert, hidebound.

(Answer: a bookworm)

Romances

Found in all languages, in both prose and verse, these long stories of brave *gestes*, or adventures, of heroes and heroines are the most typical of all medieval tales.

El Cid Among the most famous romances is the Spanish *Cid* (pronounced Sid), written in the twelfth century. *Cid* is from the Arabic word, *sidi*, which means *lord*. The poem's hero is the historic knight Rodrigo Diaz de Vivar, and its story tells of his successful battles and varied adventures in Spain and Morocco.

Song of Roland The twelfth-century French *Song of Roland (Chanson de Roland)* tells a true story of a defeat suffered by Charlemagne's army in 778, as they were returning north over the Pyrenees from Spain. At the pass of Roncevalles, also called Roncevaux, Roland and his friend Oliver are in charge of the rearguard, but are treacherously attacked by Ganelon, Roland's stepfather. Soon all but sixty of their men lie dead or dying, and Oliver urges Roland to sound his horn to bring help from Charlemagne. Roland proudly refuses until Oliver, too, is felled. Mortally wounded, Roland makes a supreme effort to sound his horn, and dies in the attempt. But he is heard by Charlemagne, who returns and avenges the betrayal.

Morte d'Arthur Even though the historical Arthur was probably a sixth-century Welsh chieftain, about whom almost nothing is known (see Chapter Four), the literary Arthur who flourishes in our imaginations is a creation of the later Middle Ages. Medieval poets wrote of him in French and German, and in English the best-known version of his stories comes at the end of the Middle Ages, in the fifteenth-century Sir Thomas Malory's prose romance, *Le Morte d'Arthur*, or *Death of Arthur*.

Malory tells a whole series of stories in his book, including Arthur's birth and his pulling the sword Excalibur from the stone; the founding of the order of Knights of the Round Table; Sir Galahad's quest for the Holy Grail, the cup from which Christ drank at the Last Supper; and the destructive love of Lancelot and Guinevere. These stories have unending appeal: in our own day, they have been made into the Lerner and Loew musical *Camelot*, the Disney movie *The Sword in the Stone*, and T. H. White's novel, *The Once and Future King*.

Sir Gawain and the Green Knight One of the greatest of the Arthurian romances, *Sir Gawain and the Green Knight* is unusual in having a clear structure, and a definite moral: honesty pays. It is also delightfully written, with wonderful descriptions of winter landscape, castle life, and festive ceremonies of feasting and the hunt. If a class were to read a single romance, this would be the one to choose. Unfortunately, it was written in the fourteenth century in a difficult Middle English dialect, much harder for modern readers than Chaucer's, and must be read in translation. Fortunately, several versions are available.

At Christmas, Sir Gawain accepts a challenge from an unknown knight dressed in green. He may strike a blow at the Green Knight, but must allow the Green Knight to strike him in turn a year later. Gawain beheads the Green Knight, who cheerily picks up his head and walks off with it. A year later, Gawain rides to the appointed place to receive his blow. But first he is invited to stay at the noble Lord Bercilak's castle, where he and the lord must exchange each evening anything they have received during the day.

Bercilak goes hunting each day, and each evening gives Gawain the game he has caught. The first day a deer, the second a wild boar, and the third a fox. Gawain has spent the days dallying with Lord Bercilak's wife who attempts to seduce him. Gawain resists her for the first and second days, and in the evening faithfully gives Bercilak the kisses he has received, but on the third day his courage fails. Knowing he must soon meet the Green Knight, he accepts from the lady a silk sash which she assures him will keep him from harm.

When the time comes, Gawain stands to receive an axe blow from the Green Knight. Thrice he is struck. The first two blows do him no harm, but the third draws blood from a small gash on his neck. The blows correspond to his dealings with Lord Bercilak: because he was faithful for two days, so the first two blows do him no harm. But because he was deceitful in a minor way on the third day, he receives a small wound. The Green Knight then reveals that he is, of course, Bercilak under an enchantment from Morgan la Fee. Gawain returns to Camelot where the knights and ladies of the Round Table agree to wear green sashes in future in his honor.

Ballads of Robin Hood Unlike the courtly Arthurian stories, read and recited in lordly castles, the stories of Robin Hood and his Merry Men are folk ballads, sung at fairs and taverns by minstrels for the entertainment of peasants and artisans. More than thirty short lively ballads tell of these outlaws who trick the rich and help the humble. Set in the twelfth century during the Crusades, the hero of these tales is Robin Hood, a nobleman wrongfully deprived of his inheritance, who lived in the forest of Sherwood with his beloved Maid Marian, Little John and his band of bowmen, and the jolly Friar Tuck, all united in an unending series of skirmishes with their enemy the Sheriff of

Nottingham. Some versions of the tales link Robin's fortunes to King Richard the Lionheart, so that when Richard is released from captivity and returned to his kingdom, Robin is returned to his rightful lands and position.

Dante's Divine Comedy Dante Alighieri (1265-1321) was a native of Florence, Italy, whose great poem, the *Divine Comedy*, celebrates his love for his city and his hatred for some of her politicians. Expelled from Florence in 1301 on political charges, Dante wrote the Comedy during his remaining years of exile in other Italian cities.

The Divine Comedy is an allegorical poem in three parts: Hell, Purgatory and Paradise. It tells of the poet, who while wandering in a dark wood, is taken by a guide, the ancient Roman poet Virgil, on a tour of Hell and Purgatory, where he encounters figures from history and his own day, suffering a variety of horrible tortures for their sins. The sinners are graded by the degree of their wickedness, and their punishment suits their crime. Hypocrites for ever wear golden cloaks lined with lead, for instance, while those who have caused discord are continuously cut in half by a demon's sword.

Finally Dante reaches the edge of the mount of Paradise, where Virgil vanishes to be replaced as a guide by Dante's lost love, Beatrice. Beatrice leads him through the nine spheres of heaven, finally showing him a vision of God's goodness. The poem's strengths include the breadth of its comprehension of an entire system of philosophy and theology, the vividness of its descriptions of people and events, and the unforgettable power of its images, all written in clear powerful Italian verse.

Fables

Poems and stories with animal characters were popular throughout the Middle Ages. The ancient fables of Aesop were among the books printed by England's first printer, William Caxton (1421-1491). Chaucer's *Nun's Priest's Tale of the Cock and Hen, Chauntecleer and Pertelote*, is a fable, as is his *Parliament of Fowls*. Fables tell tales with a moral: and the Middle Ages loved literature that taught good and evil.

Chaucer's Canterbury Tales Geoffrey Chaucer (1343?-1400) was a London merchant and court functionary who wrote *The Canterbury Tales* over many years filled with business and travel. The unfinished work is a series of poems and tales told by the members of a group of pilgrims who join together to make the popular journey to Canterbury Cathedral to pray at the tomb of St. Thomas a Beckett, the twelfth-century archbishop murdered at the desire of King Henry II.

The pilgrims represent a wide range of medieval society, including a knight and squire, nuns, monks, a jolly townswoman, and craftsmen, and the stories they tell to pass the time on their way include romances, bawdy tavern tales and pious legends. Humorous and sensitive, these tales give a closer look at medieval life than can be found in any other medieval writings. *The Nun's Priest's Tale of the Cock and Hen* is an entertaining fable that makes a good introduction to Chaucer.

Christine de Pisan One of the most famous medieval women writers was Christine de Pisan (or Pizan, 1364-1431?). Brought up at the French court and well educated, Christine was widowed early, and supported her children by writing and translating books for noble patrons. Her books include a treatise on knightly behavior, translated into English and printed by Caxton in 1489 as *The Book of Fayttes of Armes and of Chivalrye*, and *The Treasure of the City of Ladies*, a comprehensive book on proper behavior for royal and noble ladies, which ranges from etiquette to extremely practical advice, such as that the lady should always walk on the ramparts of her castle very early in the morning, so the peasants working her lands will know they must be out in the fields at dawn or their lady will notice they are slacking. Despite the need to please her patrons, Christine expressed an unorthodox feminism; her books reflect broad sympathy with the talents and achievements of women in different situations and classes. At the end of her life, while living in retirement in a convent, she even wrote a poem in support of Joan of Arc.

Mystery Plays

Mystery plays suggest Agatha Christie and Raymond Chandler, but the medieval mystery play was actually a religious play put on by the members of a trade guild. *Mystere* was Old French for a *trade*, or *profession*, and the *mystery play* was a production staged and acted by different guilds - the armorers put on the Expulsion of Adam and Eve from Eden, and made a handsome sword for the angel to drive them forth, the shipwrights presented a play about Noah's Ark, because they were able to build an impressive ark for the production, and the bakers staged the Last Supper, complete with loaves of bread.

The plays were often presented on wagons drawn through the streets, so a series of plays could be shown in succession to an audience seated at squares and open spaces along the way. Guild records show large sums of money being spent on these pageant wagons and their costumes and props. The language of the mystery plays was colloquial, and their intent was the same as that of many other kinds of medieval art — to present stories from the bible and lives of the saints to an illiterate audience in a form they could understand and enjoy.

Humor enlivens the plays — the shrewishness of Noah's wife, for example, suggests much later popular drama. The craftsmen wrote their plays themselves, adding legendary incidents and imagined details to the scriptural stories.

Other mystery plays present the Creation, the sacrifice of Abraham and Isaac, the shepherds journey to the Nativity, the Crucifixion, the Resurrection and the Day of Judgment. The English mystery plays were often presented on the feast of Corpus Christi, in late May or early June, when the weather was good. Modern versions of some of these plays, including *The Play of Daniel* and *The Play of Herod* are occasionally presented and are available on records.

Lays

Short verse romances, the most famous lays are those of Marie de France, a twelfth-century noblewoman about whose life nothing certain is known. Many of the dozen lays she wrote in Old French feature characters from the Arthurian legend and are set in Brittany or other Celtic lands, like the lay summarized here. These short songs were very suitable for troubadours to sing at dinners in castle halls.

The Lay of the Honeysuckle Sir Tristan, one of the knights of the Round Table, had been separated from his beloved Queen Iseult by order of her husband, King Mark, who was Tristan's uncle. Heartbroken at his banishment, Tristan returned to Wales and lived alone in the forest.

Hearing from a peasant that King Mark and the court would be passing through on their way to keep court at Tintagel, Tristan cut a hazel branch and peeled its bark, carving his name on the smooth wood. He placed the branch with his name showing along the main path through the forest, and waited to see what would befall.

Sure enough, the court came riding through the forest. No one noticed Tristan's branch until Queen Iseult came by, but she spotted it at once. Calling to the knights and ladies who accompanied her, she said they should dismount and take a rest. Then accompanied only by her trusted maid Brangwaine she withdrew into the forest, and found Tristan.

When it was time for Iseult to return, Tristan wept as he embraced her, saying they two were like the hazel tree and the honeysuckle vine, which twine together and flourish in the forest. But if either is rooted out or pulled up, they both wither and die. After their parting, Iseult worked to bring about a reconciliation between King Mark and Sir Tristan, and Tristan, who was a skilled harper, wrote and sang a new lay, *The Lay of the Honeysuckle.*

Activities

11-1. Latin Now

In western Europe during the Middle Ages, no matter what language you spoke at home, at school you were taught to read, write and speak Latin. We still use many Latin words today. Can you guess how many of these words are Latin? They all are! Make up a story using as many of these words as possible:

> Senator - Circus - Exhibit - Premium - Super - Doctor
> Curriculum - Villa - Forum - Video - Superior - Rumor

11-2. Riddles

Divide the class into teams. Each team makes up three verse riddles about any topic, and tries to baffle the rest of the class. Copy the Old English verse form of an alliterative half-line with four stresses in each line.

11-3. Present a Modern Mystery Play

Write a modern mystery play, with a moral, and present it - on a cart, outdoors during a medieval fair? or before a feast? This could be a multicultural experience, set in a town among diverse cultural groups.

11-4. Write a Medieval Letter

Medieval letters were very formal. Even a child writing to a parent, or a wife to her husband, began and ended with protestations of respect. "Right worshipful and my own True Husband, I commend me to your care." Suppose you are one of Christine de Pisan's children, sent away to school. Let her know how your life is. Try to convince her to let you visit a friend during the summer vacation. How will you travel to your friend's house? Will you go alone, or in a group of pilgrims? How long will the journey take?

11-5. Write a Fable or a Lay

11-6. Write a New Canterbury Tales

Each student will choose a character to go on pilgrimage to Camelot, Canterbury, Jerusalem or any other medieval destination. Describe your character, and write a poem or story that your character would enjoy telling.

Make a book with all the stories written nicely in script, and illuminated.

11-7. Write an adventure story (a "romance") about King Arthur or some other medieval character.

Vocabulary Words for Chapter Eleven

old wives' tales	Middle English
romance	alliteration
Old English	ballad
Anglo-Saxon	allegory
sabaton	fable
gorget	mystery play
gauntlet	lay

Chapter Twelve

The Grand Finale: A Medieval Festival

Festival Options — In increasing order of complexity! Any or all of these events can be combined. . . .

A Day at the Tournament

Tournament The easiest culminating activity is an Academic Tournament. This can be held in the classroom, in about two class periods. Small prizes should be given to the winning teams: reproduction medieval coins are particularly appropriate, or small toy knights, or dragons, or medieval-looking costume jewelry.

Make a Tournament Tree Lords who wished to hold a tournament would send their heralds far and wide with a proclamation announcing the time, place and rules of the tournament.
At the chosen field, a large tree was often designated the Tournament Tree. Knights who wished to participate would hang their shields on this.
A classroom tree can be painted on brown paper, 7 feet high, cut out and pinned to a bulletin board. Shields or banners can then be thumb-tacked to the tree to announce the start of the tournament.

Four Jousts The class may be divided into teams, for a *melee*, or work individually, for a *joust*. At the end of the four events, scores are totted up and winners proclaimed, who could then be honored by being chosen as Lords and Ladies to preside at the High Table at a Medieval Feast.

1. Riddling Joust or Melee
Make up puns or riddles on medieval topics and see who can solve them.
Examples:
Which famous castle is like a desert parking lot?
Answer: Camelot.

What did the knight say to the herald when he came to order his coat-of-arms?
Answer: Charge it.

2. Canting Joust or Melee *(See illustration of canting arms on page 39.)*
Draw *canting arms* for well-known legendary or real people.
Whoever guesses the answer first, wins.

3. Rhyming Joust or Melee
Make up questions with rhyming answers.
Example:
What piece of armor can be made from wood whose bark has been peeled?
Answer: A shield.

4. Questing Joust or Melee ➡

4. Questing Joust or Melee
Make up questions on medieval life and culture.
Examples:
What group invaded England in 1066?
Answer: Duke William and his Norman knights.

Which famous lady is said to have jousted?
Answer: Queen Eleanor of Aquitaine.

Medieval Games

Life-size chess This game may be set up in the parking lot or gymnasium. Other ancient games such as checkers, blind man's buff and fives may be set up at small tables around the chess board.

Chess is an ancient game based on warfare in India. It was very popular in medieval Europe, and was played by knights and ladies in every country. The chessmen represent a medieval army, with its king, queen, bishops, knights, castles (rooks), and peasants (pawns).

To hold a life-size chess match: Paint a checkered pattern on the playground, with 64 squares, each 18-24 inches across arranged in 8 rows of 8 squares each. Indoors, the squares may be outlined with masking tape, or by sewing together one king and three twin sheets, with 20 inch squares marked in alternate paint.

Either:
Make large chess men, 2 feet high, from posterboard and papier mache. These will be moved at each turn by some appointed players.

Or:
Make tabards from burlap or old sheets to identify the students who will play the "chess men". One team should be in a dark color, and one in a light. Cut the tabards according to the pattern for Tunics in Chapter Eight, ending them at the hips or just above the knee. Decorate the tabards with paint or cut-out patterns on the chest and upper back: a crown for the king and queen, a cross for bishops, crossed swords for the knights, and towers for the castles.

Appoint two game-masters, who sit at the side and decide their team's move, with advice from the onlookers! The game-masters can see the board better if they are seated on a ladder or raised chair. *(For other medieval games, see Chapter Four)*

A Medieval Play

Play or Entertainment This can be held at an assembly before the whole school, with or without parents. It can consist of a short play written by the students, with music, poems, stories, jokes, riddles, juggling, tumbling or dances — all with a medieval theme — performed by a roster of troubadours, musicians, pilgrims, jesters and jugglers.

A Medieval Fair

Fairs were the most important commercial events in the Middle Ages, comparable to trade shows today. They were also exciting social events. Fairs were held in towns and cities, some of which built permanent fair-grounds. They were also held at important cross-roads on major routes used by merchants, and some cities were later established at these fair sites.

How to Hold a Fair

Fair Day This can be either an indoor or outdoor event, in playground, auditorium or gymnasium, lasting half a day.

A town often indicated it was holding a fair by hanging a *white glove* over the town gates. A real glove, plumped up with crumpled paper, or a papier mache glove, can be fixed on a dowel and hung over the classroom door.

Entertainers appear among the crowd or on stage; wandering minstrels, jugglers, tumblers, magicians and storytellers. A guild might decide to stage a Mystery Play at the fair *(see Chapters 3 and 11)* . Fortune tellers can ply their trade. They should be set up in a dimly lighted booth. Their clients must cross their palms with silver; the seers read fortune-cooky fortunes that everyone in the school has saved throughout this unit. Medieval games may be played *(see page 90)*.

Merchants offering rare goods from far and near are the heart of the fair: they should dress appropriately, and offer goods from the lands they come from or have visited. The merchants can be set up simply at tables, or more ambitiously, stalls can be made for them from appliance boxes with cut-outs forming a counter.

Merchants and craftspeople at the fair can include:

Scribes — selling beautifully-written poems, or short stories.
Illuminators — offering to write and decorate a visitor's monogram.
Heralds — selling and custom-designing heraldic pennants and coats-of-arms.
Tailors — selling hennins and other hats.
Cooks — selling spice cookies.
Butlers — offering spiced punch.
Jewelers — offering beautiful beach stones, or small pieces of minerals.
Herb sellers — offering fresh or dried herbs.
Spice merchants — offering small packets of kitchen spices.

Appropriate snacks and beverages may be sold: profits might be used toward a class fieldtrip. Other goods offered could be papier mache replicas, of silver salt cellars or goblets, for example, or clay gargoyles or mirrors *(see Chapter 10)* . Use the information on the maps in this book to choose goods and sources.

Visitors: Pilgrims might wander the crowd, telling of the marvels they have seen and requesting alms. Nobles from the local castle stroll in the crowd, shopping and enjoying the entertainment, as do craftsmen from the town, peasants and yeomen from the manor farm, and even a few monks or nuns from the monastery.

How to Hold a Medieval Feast

Feast The perfect ending to a medieval tournament, play or fair day! With the food cooked at home ahead of time, and heated up in borrowed micro-wave ovens or large pots, this is not too difficult. The entertainment is as important as the food, and each course should be followed by one of the activities listed under "Plays" above. This takes about two hours, and should be held in a cafeteria decorated with the students' heraldry and artwork.

Feasts were even more enjoyable in the Middle Ages than today, because so many people then knew what it was to feel hungry. Still, to celebrate a wedding, or festival like Christmas or Easter, or the coronation of a king, wonderful great banquets were prepared. Everyone dressed in their best clothes, troubadours, musicians, dancers and jugglers entertained, and for a while young and old forgot their cares and were merry.

Decorating and Cooking

Decorating the Hall The lord and lady presiding should sit at the end of the hall, preferably at a "high table", one raised above the others. A cloth hanging behind their chairs indicates their importance. Heraldic banners or shields should hang around the walls. See the drawing of a medieval banquet here for ideas.

Cloths should cover the tables. "Saltcellars," tall silver-colored goblets, should stand on the High Table: they may be made from papier mache.

Goblets and knives and loaves of bread should be on the table at the start of the meal.

Cooking Techniques Medieval cookery is primarily open-hearth cooking. Most houses did not have ovens, so cooks prepared food by boiling it in iron pots hung over the hearth, or roasting it on spits or skewers. Stews were braised in a small amount of liquid in pots. However, baked foods, breads and pies, were very popular. Noble people in castles and great manor houses did have ovens and their cooks baked at home, while humble people without ovens sent out to bakers, and either purchased their pies and breads, or paid to have their prepared dough baked for them.

Table Manners Table-manners, though different from ours, were taken seriously and several books were written on them. Hands were washed at the start and end of a meal, since food was eaten with the fingers. Only the right hand was used to take food from the common serving bowl, and only the first three fingers were used to carry food to the mouth. Young boys of the household, pages and squires, served their elders, carving meat and passing dishes and jugs. Diners were urged not to wipe their hands on their dogs, who sat under the table awaiting scraps.

Banquet Furnishings Banners and canopies decorated the walls, especially behind the High Table where the lord and lady presided. The High Table was often on a raised dais, but all tables were set up on trestles, and covered with fine linen cloths. Kings and great lords ate off plates of precious gold or silver. Yeomen and prosperous peasants had wooden plates, while most simple people had no plates at all, but ate off thick slices of stale bread called *trenchers*. These sopped up gravy, and were eaten at the end of the meal by people or dogs. Since eating with the fingers can be messy, start the meal by having the servers tie large linen or cotton napkins around the diners' necks.

Forks were unknown until the end of the Middle Ages, when they reached the west from Venice. Diners brought their own knives to table, and were given a spoon. Salt cellars were large covered chalices, often of silver, as befitted the value of the commodity, and were placed on the high table near the important people; humble folk sat *below the salt*. Goblets were as fine as could be afforded. Silver or gold cups or *mazers* were often given as gifts by royal people, while ordinary people had pewter or wooden cups.

Serving the Meal

Grace The meal begins with the ceremonial arrival of the grand people who will sit at the High Table. All stand until the lord bids them be seated. Grace should be said by a designated "monk", or by all the diners. It may be very simple: Thanks be to God for all his blessings. Response: Amen.

The Toast The lord stands, and is followed by the whole assembly. All hold up in their right hand a glass containing anything but water, which negates a toast. The lord offers the old toast: *Wassail!* (Pronounced wass-hale.) "Wassail" derives from the Old English phrase *waes hael*, which means *Be well.* To which the guests may reply, *Drink hale!*

Finger Bowls Then pages called *ewerers* will bring bowls of spiced water and towels in which all the diners wash their fingers. *Panters* (bread servers) then carve the trenchers of bread and place one in front of each diner. While the butlers pour the beverage, minstrels entertain, as they will between each course.

Banquet Entertainment

Musicians played trumpets and lutes throughout the meal. Each *remove* (course) was announced by the trumpeters. In modern times, a tape player can supply background music, but live songs, and if possible, instrumental music by recorders, drums or any other instrument, add greatly to the atmosphere.

Between removes, a group of six or eight diners can entertain their fellows with a round dance. Juggling, tumbling, riddles and stories are all appropriate. All of the diners should entertain in some fashion during the meal. Non-performers may tell a story of some recent event, perhaps an adventure such as that of Sir Gawain at the Chapel of the Green Knight, or Sir Tristan's encounter with Queen Iseult in the greenwood. *(See Chapter 11)*

Before any food is served to the guests, it is tried by the King's Taster, who is watched carefully to see if he turns color or falls in a faint. Once he pronounces a food good, the *carvers* then serve it to the presiding king and queen, or lord and lady, and then to the rest of the guests.

Toward the end of the meal, the king may call on the guests to see if anyone there has a marvel to tell. Finally, grace is said again, and the people from the High Table leave in procession.

Medieval Food Facts to Bear in Mind

Food was local — It was grown in nearby gardens, raised in surrounding farms, or foraged or hunted in neighboring forests.

Spices were an exception — They were brought by merchants from Asia, Africa and the Near East so people in northern Europe could enjoy cinnamon, ginger, nutmeg and many more — if they could afford them.

Herbs and spices were used in every dish, if available: they added the high flavors relished by medieval diners, disguised food that was rancid or spoiled, and were believed to be of great help in maintaining the diners' health.

Fruits were also imported — So English people could sometimes enjoy lemons, oranges, figs and dates brought from the Mediterranean countries or even farther.

Food was seasonal — Medieval people had no refrigerators, freezers, or chemical preservatives except salt. To preserve food, they salted it or dried it. Farm animals were slaughtered in late fall, when fodder died out, and the meat salted for winter and spring use. Salt was a vital necessity in the Middle Ages. The only fresh meat available in the winter was that brought back by hunters. Apples, cabbages and root vegetables were stored over winter in a cool place; dried fruits such as raisins and prunes were also popular.

Fast Days were many — Medieval society was intensely religious, and the church forbade the eating of meat on many *fast days*. *Advent*, the three week period before Christmas, and *Lent*, the six weeks before Easter, were the longest periods of fasting. If possible, avoid holding your feast during Advent or Lent, or serve a non-meat main dish. Fish, eggs, cheese and legumes were the main dishes served on fast days — castles and monasteries had fish ponds where live fish were held until needed.

Anything edible was eaten — Because of the endemic food shortage, many surprising creatures were eaten, including peacock and swan, both of which were highly prized as delicacies.

No American foods were available to medieval Europeans! — The existence of America was unknown until Columbus' great voyage in 1492, at the end of the period.

Foods never seen on the medieval table — include bananas, cane sugar, chocolate, coffee, corn, ice-cream, peanuts, pecans, pineapples, potatoes, tea, tomatoes and turkey.

Foods for an Authentic Simple Medieval Feast from Northern Europe

Soups Barley, beef, borscht, cabbage, chicken, mutton broth, Scotch broth. Drink it from pottery bowls, or use a wooden spoon. Serve with round loaves of crusty bread. (If you use wooden spoons, give them as a souvenir to the feasters - they cannot easily be sterilized.)

Meats *Viands*. Beef tenderloin tips or chicken wings and drumsticks are easy to eat with the fingers — forks did not come into use until after the Middle Ages. Meats were often prepared with nuts and dried fruits, raisins or prunes. Meat pies were also popular, and can be eaten with a knife and spoon. Serve from a large wooden tray, such as a bread-board, or a bowl. Serve on trenchers — thick slices of stale or toasted crusty bread. Accompany with fresh crusty bread, sliced from a round loaf by the guests or a server.

Vegetables Year round — beans, beetroot, cabbage, carrots, leeks, onions, parsnips, dried peas, rice (which they imported), turnips. Seasonal - fresh peas or asparagus in spring, lettuce in late spring and summer. Serve from a large pottery bowl, eat in the soup bowls.

Salads Any of these vegetables, if in season or dried, could be used. Medieval salads often used nuts (filberts, hazelnuts or walnuts), fruit and vegetables together, in colorful compositions sometimes resembling a coat-of-arms or a landscape. Sprinkle plenty of fresh herbs on top. In season, edible flowers can be used to decorate a salad: violets, nasturtiums and calendula or "Pot Marigolds" — make sure the flowers have not been chemically sprayed. A Waldorf salad of apples, walnuts and shredded carrot is a good approximation, although in medieval times fruits and vegetables were rarely eaten raw, so it would be more correct if the apple and carrot were lightly cooked. Arrange the salad on a tray, or in a large shallow bowl; eat from the soup bowls. Before arranging the salad, toss the vegetables in a dressing of cider, honey, mustard and herbs.

Herbs/Spices Chervil, cinnamon, garlic, ginger, honey for sweetening, mint, mustard, parsley, pepper, rosemary, sage, salt, thyme, vinegar. Medieval food was highly spiced — sometimes to disguise the taste of meat past its prime! Sweet and sour combinations were popular.

Cheese Cream cheese, ricotta, cottage cheese or farmer's cheese, plain or sweetened with honey, can be served as dessert or as part of the main course.

Dessert Almond, gingerbread or spice cookies or cakes. Plum or cherry cake. Apple or pear pies. Local berries in season, with cream (not ice-cream!). Nutcake. Custards. Custard pudding with raisins or mint. Shortbread. Cheesecake. Jellies. Serve on a fresh trencher, or from a clean bowl.

Beverages Cider, apple- or grape-juice, or non-alcoholic "mead" made by stirring a tablespoon of honey into a quart of cider. Red berry punch, imitating wine or "Hyppocras", a strained spiced wine. Hot mulled cider. Most medieval drinks were alcoholic, an effective way of preserving them beyond harvest time. Ale, hard cider and perry (made from pears) were most popular, followed by mead, made from fermented honey often flavored with apples. The rich drank wine. If possible, serve in a goblet of wood, pewter, pottery or glass — an inexpensive sundae glass, or colored glass vase. Beverages are served from large pitchers by *butlers*.

Medieval Recipes: A Simple Medieval Menu for Modern Tastes

First Remove
Potage or Broth
Rastons

Second Remove
Rosted Fowle
Legume Spears
Salat

Third Remove
Gelye
Tarte of Chese
Soteltes
Ypocras

Recipes continued ➡

Recipes

Potage or Broth - Cream of vegetable or chicken soup, served in bowls.

Rastons — Originally a stuffed herbed bread. Use onion or poppyseed rolls.

Rosted Fowle — Chicken, baked or roasted with garlic and/or herbs, and served in easy-to-eat sized pieces as finger food.

Legume Spears — Carrots, celery or parsnips, or a mixture of these, cut in 4-inch sticks and braised in broth. Do not overcook: they will be picked up and eaten with the fingers, and should be crisp.

Salat — Toss finely shredded red cabbage in a Dijon mustard or spicy peppercorn dressing. Arrange on a platter with sliced apples, pears, almonds and walnuts.

Gelye — Lemon or berry jelly, with cream if desired, served in a clean bowl.

Tarte of Chese — Cheese cake, plain or with cherry or other seasonal berry sauce.

Soteltes — Subtleties, or Little Surprises: almonds or filberts wrapped in dates or prunes.

Ypocras — Spiced wine. Use cider or red punch with mulling spices or a little cinnamon.

Vocabulary Words for Chapter Twelve

trenchers
mazers
high table
wassail
panters
removes
viands
potage
soteltes
ypocras
gelye
fowle

EMBLEMS FOR TIMELINE ACTIVITY

KINGS & QUEENS & HEROES

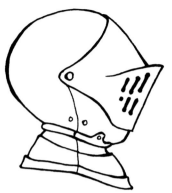

POLITICAL & SOCIAL EVENTS

RELIGIOUS FIGURES & EVENTS

DISCOVERY & SCIENCE

WRITERS & BOOKS

ART & MUSIC

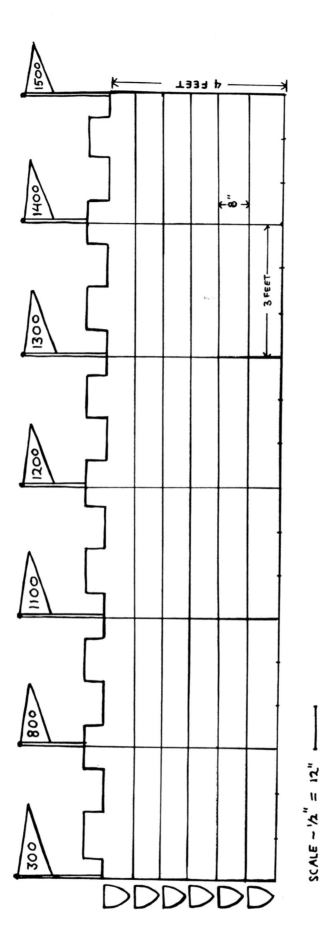

SCALE ~ ½" = 12"

Chapter Thirteen

Timeline & Vocabulary Activities

Timeline Activity

The castle wall chart *(on the lefthand page, 96b)* represents a blank Middle Ages timeline. The flags on the top of the wall mark off the centuries from A.D. 300-1500.

The wall is divided into six horizontal rows, with a shield marking each row at the left end of the wall. Each row represents a different area of medieval life, indicated by the emblem *(see emblems on page 96a)* on the appropriate shield. From top to bottom , we have . . .

Category:	Emblem:
Kings, Queens & Heroes	*Crown*
Political & Social Events	*Helmet*
Religious Figures & Events	*Church*
Discovery & Science	*Sailing ship*
Writers & Books	*Open book*
Art & Music	*Lute & paint brush*

How to make the timeline:
1. Redraw the wall on brown wrapping paper or craft paper, as large as you wish, and fix it on the wall or bulletin board.
2. Make six small shields from different colored construction paper, sized to fit on each of the six rows on your wall. Choose one color for each of the six rows.
3. Photocopy each emblem (helmet, crown, etc. on page 96a), cut them out, and glue each one to one of the paper shields.
4. Glue the shields to the left side of the wall, indicating the category of event to be noted in each row: the crown on the top row for *Kings, Queens & Heroes*; the helmet on the second row from the top for *Political & Social Events*; and so on down to the lute & paint brush on the bottom row.
5. Make six copies of each emblem, and glue them on appropriate colored paper shields.
6. Each student chooses an emblem and writes an item for the timeline, with name and date, on the shield.
7. Pin the shields on the timeline at the appropriate date and line.

Vocabulary Columns Activity

All new words encountered in this unit should be written by the students on tall columns of 12 inch wide paper hung on the walls at regular intervals, like the columns supporting a Gothic building. The columns may have capitals and bases (wider projections at the top and bottom) like those on the drawing of the flying buttress. These can be cut from ends of newsprint rolls, which is often 2 feet wide and available free or very cheaply from a newspaper printer; or from a roll of craft paper.

Medieval People Mentioned in this Book

Medieval people are normally listed in encyclopedias and reference books under the initial of their first name, not their last: Thomas Aquinas is listed under *Thomas*, for example. The poet Geoffrey Chaucer is an exception. The following are listed in chronological order:

Emperor Constantine the Great of Rome (reigned 306-337)

St. Patrick (385?-461?) — converts Ireland

St. George the Dragon Slayer — Patron Saint of England (4th century)

St. Benedict of Nursia (480-543) — founder of Benedictine monasticism

Byzantine Emperor Justinian I (483-565)

Byzantine Empress Theodora (508-548)

Uther Pendragon (legendary, or perhaps 6th century) — father of King Arthur

King Arthur (probably 6th century) — legendary British hero

Queen Guinevere (probably 6th century) — King Arthur's wife

Sir Launcelot du Lac & Knights of the Round Table (legendary, or perhaps 6th century)

Pope Gregory the Great (590-604) — compiler of Gregorian chant

Caedmon (7th century) — earliest known English poet

St. Hilda (614-680) — English abbess

Venerable Bede (672-735) — English historian

Emperor Charlemagne (742-814) — French hero

Emperor Otto I (died 973) — King of the Franks & Lombards

William the Conqueror (1027?-1087) — conquered England in 1066

Leif Ericsson (flourished circa 1000) — probably reached North America from Greenland

El Cid (1045-1099) — hero of Spanish romance

Emperor Henry IV (1053-1106) — participated in Investiture Controversy

Pope Gregory VII (Hildebrand - 1073-1085) — Investiture Controversy

Abbot Suger (1081-1151) — commissioned first Gothic church

St. Bernard of Clairvaux (1090?-1153) — reforming Cistercian abbot

Queen Eleanor of Aquitaine (1122?-1204) — patron of the arts

Count Geoffrey of Anjou (died 1151) — founder of English Plantagenet dynasty

King John of England (1119-1216) — signed Magna Carta

King Louis VII of France (1137-1180) — crusader husband of Eleanor of Aquitaine

Saladin (1137?-1193) — Sultan of Egypt, opponent of crusader Richard I Lionheart

King Richard I Lionheart of England (1157-99) — crusader

Marie de France (12th century) — author of French poems

St. Dominic (1170-1221) — founder of the Dominican Friars

St. Francis (1182?-1226) — founder of Franciscan Friars & patron saint of animals

St. Albertus Magnus (1193-1280) — German scholar

Emperor Frederick II (1194-1250) — King of Sicily

St. Louis IX (1214-1270) — King of France

Roger Bacon (1214?-1294?) — English scientist

St. Thomas Aquinas (1225-1274) — Italian philosopher and theologian

Villard de Honnecourt (flourished 1230-40) — architectural and mechanical draughtsman

Marco Polo (1254?-1324?) — traveler to China

Dante Alighieri (1265-1321) — Italian poet

Giotto (1266?-1337?) — Florentine painter

Duccio di Buoninsegna (flourished 1278-1319) — Sienese painter

Geoffrey Chaucer (1343?-1400) — English poet

Richard Whittington (1358-1423) — Lord Mayor of London

Christine de Pisan (1364-1431?) — French writer

John Dunstable (1370?-1453) — English composer

Limbourg Brothers (flourished 1380-1416) — Franco-flemish manuscript illuminators

Johan Gutenberg (1397?-1468) — inventor of printing press with movable type

Fra Angelico (1400?-1450) — Florentine painter, friar

St. Joan of Arc (1412?-1431) — defender of France

William Caxton (1421-1491) — English printer

Sir Thomas Malory (died 1471) — author of *Le Morte D'Arthur*

Margaret Paston (1424?-1484) — English lady of the manor & letter-writer

Johannes Ockhegem (1425?-1495) — Flemish composer

Jacob Obrecht (1450-1505) — Flemish composer

Josquin des Pres (1450?-1521) — Flemish composer

Heinrich Isaac (1450?-1517) — Flemish composer

Nicholas Copernicus (1473-1543) — astronomer

Martin Luther (1483-1546) — religious reformer

Famous Folk

Medieval People became famous for many different reasons. See how many of these well-known people you can connect with their achievements. *(Put the achievement number on the line after the name)*

A Marco Polo ___		**1**	Conquered England
B St. George ___		**2**	Patron Saint of Animals
C Eleanor of Aquitaine ___		**3**	Traveled to North America
D King Arthur ___		**4**	Crusader
E St. Hilda ___		**5**	Wrote French Poems
F Saladin ___		**6**	Emperor of the Franks
G St. Francis ___		**7**	Traveled to China
H King Richard the Lionheart ___		**8**	Founded the Knights of the Round Table
I Roger Bacon ___		**9**	Hero of Spanish Poem
J Leif Ericsson ___		**10**	Defender of France
K Marie de France ___		**11**	English Abbess
L William the Conqueror ___		**12**	Encouraged artists
M Charlemagne ___		**13**	Dragon-slayer
N Joan of Arc ___		**14**	English scientist
O El Cid ___		**15**	Sultan of Egypt

Medieval Events Mentioned in this Book

Fall of the Roman Empire, 476

Founding of Benedictine Monasticism, 6th century

Book of Kells, circa 800

Vikings establish cities in the British Isles, 9th-10th centuries

Improved harness for horses, 9th century

Leif Ericsson reaches North America, circa 1000

Horseshoes introduced, 11th century

High-wheeled plow introduced, 11th century

Normans conquer England - Battle of Hastings, 1066

Investiture Controversy, 1076

Crusades, 1095-1291

Penance at Canossa, 1077

Earliest Gothic cathedrals —- St-Denis and Chartres, circa 1150

Oldest known heraldic coat-of-arms, 1151

First medieval universities established — Bologna, Paris, Oxford, 12th century

Children's Crusade, 1212

Magna Carta, 1215

Inquisition established in France, 1233

Transitional armor, 1250-1400

Acre fell to Muslims, 1291

Hundred Years War between France and England, 1337-1453

Black Death, or Plague, 1346-1356

Full plate armor, 1400

Paper becomes widely available in Europe, 15th century

Execution of Joan of Arc, 1431

Invention of printing press with movable type, 1436

Wars of the Roses, 1455-1485

Reunification of Spain, 1492

Expulsion of Jews from Spain, 1492

Reading List

Chapters One & Two

Calliope: World History for Young People (magazine - many issues deal with Middle Ages). Cobblestone Publishing, Peterborough, NH

Europe and the Middle Ages. Edward M. Peters. Prentice-Hall, 1988

Medieval Europe: A Short History. C. Warren Hollister. Wiley, 1974

The Middle Ages (Cambridge Introduction to World History). Trevor Cairns. Cambridge University Press, 1972

Chapter Three

Adam of the Road. Elizabeth Gray. Viking, 1942

Medieval People. Eileen Power. Doubleday Anchor

The Black Death, also *Columbus & the Age of Explorers* (historical document portfolios). Jackdaw and Golden Owl Publishing. Amawalk, NY

Two Travelers. Christopher Manson. Holt, 1990

Chapter Four

Alfred the Great, also *Magna Carta* (historical document portfolios). Jackdaw and Golden Owl Publishing. Amawalk, NY

Sir Gawain and the Green Knight. Selina Hastings. Lothrop, 1981

The Castle in the Attic. Elizabeth Winthrop. Bantam-Skylark, 1985

The Story of King Arthur and His Knights. Howard Pyle. Dover

Chapter Five

A Tournament of Knights. Joe Lasker. Crowell, 1986

Merry Ever After. Joe Lasker. Viking/Puffin, 1986

Chapter Six

Aesop's Fables. Grosset & Dunlap, 1963

Castle and *Cathedral*. David Macaulay. Houghton Mifflin, 1982 & 1981 (also available in a video version)

The Door in the Wall. Marguerite DeAngeli. Doubleday, 1949

The Spanish Inquisition (historical document portfolio). Jackdaw and Golden Owl Publishing. Amawalk, NY

Chapter Seven

A Medieval Feast. Aliki. Harper & Row, 1983

The Peasants' Revolt (historical document portfolios).
Jackdaw and Golden Owl Publishing. Amawalk, NY

The Merry Adventures of Robin Hood. Howard Pyle. Dover

Chapter Nine

Music in the Medieval World. Albert Seay. Prentice-Hall, 1975

Chapter Ten

Medieval Art: Painting, Sculpture, Architecture 4th-14th Century. James Snyder.
Prentice-Hall/Abrams, 1989

Monuments of Medieval Art. Robert G. Calkins. Dutton, 1979

Chapter Eleven

Canterbury Tales. Geoffrey Chaucer, adapted by Barbara Cohen. Lothrop, 1988

Chanticleer and the Fox. Geoffrey Chaucer. Crowell Junior Books, 1982

Proud Knight, Fair Lady: the 12 Lais of Marie de France. Naomi Lewis, translator.
Viking Kestrel, 1989

Valentine and Orson. Nancy Ekholm Burkert. Farrar, Strauss, 1984

Chapter Twelve

To the King's Taste. Lorna J. Sass. Metropolitan Museum/St. Martin's, 1975

Key to Medieval Times Word Search, page 19

```
P  O  R  T  C  U  L  L  I  S
O  T  L  A  H  M  A  C  E  I
L  L  E  P  I  E  M  A  D  R
E  I  I  E  V  X  E  G  A  P
A  T  R  S  A  L  I  A  L  F
R  H  O  T  L  T  S  U  O  J
M  G  P  T  R  O  J  A  C  K
A  I  E  R  Y  L  A  N  C  E
T  N  E  M  E  L  T  T  A  B
E  K  K  Y  L  A  D  U  E  F
```

Key to The World of Heraldry Word Search, page 41

```
E  S  C  U  T  C  H  E  O  N
C  R  O  L  O  C  E  Q  U  X
N  L  A  T  E  M  R  U  S  C
E  O  T  T  O  M  A  A  Y  R
R  E  O  N  O  I  L  R  C  E
E  G  F  I  E  L  D  T  N  S
F  R  A  R  U  F  R  E     T
F  A  R  O  S  E  Y  R  D  A
I  H  M  G  N  I  T  N  A  C
D  C  S  E  L  G  A  E  C  D
```

Key to The Monastic World Word Search, page 49

```
M  O  N  K  E  A  N  T  H  F
O  X  U  R  T  R  C  O  U  A
N  E  N  T  A  U  L  B  U  T
A  B  E  L  L  L  O  B  R  C
S  C  R  I  B  E  I  A  E  I
T  H  K  O  O  B  S  Y  T  D
E  O  H  A  B  I  T  E  P  E
R  I  B  R  E  H  E  B  A  N
Y  R  A  I  V  E  R  B  H  E
P  R  I  O  R  Y  X  A  C  B
```

Key to Medieval Art and Artists Word Search, page 79

```
M  A  N  U  S  C  R  I  P  T
E  N  S  Y  M  B  O  L  Z  V
R  O  M  A  N  E  S  Q  U  E
U  T  C  O  C  S  E  R  F  L
T  T  I  N  S  P  W  C  A  L
P  T  H  O  U  I  I  R  N  U
L  O  T  R  G  R  N  O  G  M
U  I  O  T  E  E  D  T  E  X
C  Y  G  A  R  G  O  Y  L  E
S  H  A  P  E  D  W  O  O  D
```

Maze Solution for page 34d

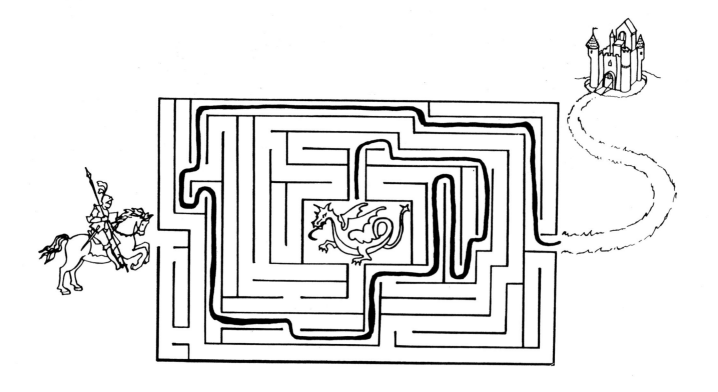

Answers to Famous Folk Activity, page 98

A - 7   I - 14
B - 13   J - 3
C - 12   K - 5
D - 8   L - 1
E - 11   M - 6
F - 15   N - 10
G - 2   O - 9
H - 4